I0570566

For my Bubbie and Pop-pop,
Renée and Horace Phillimore,
for all their encouragement.

Acknowledgments

I would like to thank my mother, Maxine Wittman, and my father, Jack Hewitt, for always providing support to me and my endeavors.

A special thanks to the artist who lent her creativity to this project, Darah Sueme, and to editor Laura Markowitz.

And Other Stories

By Kerri A. Hewitt

Story Bridge Books
2013

Copyright © Kerri A. Hewitt, 2013
ISBN: 978-0-9849164-6-7

All rights reserved.

Illustrations by Darah Sueme

Cover design by Michael Leclair

Without limiting the rights under copyright reserved above, no part of this publication may be reproduced, stored in or introduced into a retrieval system, or transmitted, in any form, or by any means (electronic, mechanical, photocopying, recording, or otherwise), without the prior written permission of the copyright owner.

This is a work of fiction. Names, characters, places and incidents are the product of the author's imagination. Any resemblances to actual persons, living or dead, business, establishments, events or locales is entirely coincidental.

If you like this book, tell your friends! For comments, questions and more information about upcoming books by Kerri Hewitt, visit www.storybridgebooks.com

Thanks for reading!

Story Bridge Books
2013

Table of Contents

The Office Worker Meets the Artist

The most important day of my life? Yes, I remember that day quite clearly. You see, that was the day I met the artist.

It was a Tuesday, a completely and utterly normal Tuesday, and I was on my way to work. So there I was, waiting impatiently at my bus stop, when a frog hopped up beside me. I was more than a bit startled as this was no ordinary frog. Most frogs are some shade of brownish green—somewhere between the bark of a tree and the leaves that decorate that same tree. This one, however, was bright, neon green.

At first, I thought the frog must have been some product of radiation poisoning, which wouldn't have surprised me in the least given all the chemicals in the water nowadays. I stared at the frog and the frog stared right back at me, not moving. I thought it might be safe to venture in a little bit closer. I inched toward it, but the damn thing frightened easily. It hopped right into the street, where it was promptly run over by nine of the 18 wheels of a semi truck.

Then my bus arrived. Frankly, I was relieved to get away from the murder scene. I've never been much of a fan of road kill. Now I know that if I hadn't gotten on that bus at that moment, I would have seen something where there was once a squashed frog that would have surprised me greatly.

I usually like to read on the way to work, but on that Tuesday I couldn't concentrate. When I can't concentrate or I'm not awake enough to read I simply stare out the window. I've always enjoyed watching scenery quickly pass before my eyes. As we drove through the city, I admired the murals painted on the sides of the buildings. I have always been a fan of murals. Blank walls are so uninspired. We approached one of my favorites, which had been there for as long as I can remember. It was a painting of a man and a woman— each holding an umbrella—walking across the wall, yet making no progress at all. Usually, when my bus drove past I tried to glimpse it so that I could note the lack of progress the couple had made.

But that morning, something was different. Instead of being frozen at the far left edge of the wall, the couple had somehow moved all the way to the right, as if they had indeed walked across the wall. And for a second I almost thought I saw the woman laugh.

I blinked and we sped past the couple. I craned my neck for a second look, but no luck; the wall was out of my sight. I rubbed my eyes. The figures in the mural couldn't possibly have walked across the wall. Art doesn't move, I told myself.

I decided I must not have gotten enough sleep the night before, or maybe it was the fumes from the paint and new carpet at work that were making me see things. Management had been doing a lot of remodeling in the building, and although they insisted there was no harm in inhaling the off-gasses and other chemicals, my coworkers and I had begun to wonder.

Yes, I worked in an office. I'm not going to say exactly which office, but let's just say that it was no different from all the other offices in my city. We may have had a different name and made different products than our neighbors, but in the end it seemed to me the people, the products and the purpose were all the same. It was all just one big, boring bureaucracy of paperwork and spreadsheets.

With the jaded mindset that could only have developed after years of shuffling useless papers from one pile to another, I climbed the four stories to my floor and quietly sat down at my cubicle. I was senior enough to have a desk with a window in the corner of the floor, so it wasn't as bad as it could have been. The wooden desk's surface was covered with a fresh mound of what promised to be a whole day's worth of highly tedious forms to fill out. I picked up my pen and resigned myself to another eight hours of utter monotony.

I had long ago covered the faces of my clocks and the corner of my computer screen with duct tape in order to avoid spending painstaking minute after minute urging the clock forward. Therefore, I was surprised when my boss, Sherri, popped in to tell me to take my lunch break. In fact, I was so surprised that I almost didn't remember to hide the sketch of the frog I'd been drawing on a sticky note. Before Sherri could see it, I slid it underneath the important document I was pretending to work on.

My wife had recently begun to take a women's empowerment class—a class I had been all in favor of until the professor told her that packing one's lazy husband's lunch every day was a sign of subservience rather than an act of love. Since I had not the teaspoon of talent that my wife did in the kitchen, I headed out the door to find a bite to eat. I tried not to linger on memories of homemade baked ziti and peanut butter and jelly sandwiches with the crusts neatly cut off.

I stopped halfway down the block, despite my stomach's grumbling protests, when I noticed something odd about the mural on the side of the café across the street. I had always liked that one. It looked like it could be the fantasy world of a seven-year-old girl. There was a brightly colored rainbow stretching across the sky, with black musical notes playing in the background to large, blooming flowers and purple and pink butterflies. It was one of the butterflies that caught my attention. I could have sworn it was moving, that the tip of its wing fluttered out from the concrete wall on which it was painted. But that was impossible, of course. So I crossed the street and peered closely at the mural. Nothing moved. I leaned closer and closer until my nose nearly grazed the butterfly's abdomen.

At that moment, the butterfly peeled itself off the wall. It placed one and then the other of its thin, black legs on the bridge of my nose. This was no small butterfly. It spread its purple and black wings, which reached past the ends of my ears. I dared not move, although I wasn't afraid. For a moment, we both froze in our close proximity, and then the butterfly took off. I turned my face to the sky and watched as it flapped higher and higher until it was nothing more than a bright purple speck. It could have been a balloon, a kite, a bird or a faraway airplane.

I stood there staring into the sky until an angry-looking older man bumped into me and knocked me to the ground. I shook my head and got back to my feet. I ignored the man's invectives and scrutinized the mural. Where there had once been a purple butterfly frolicking under the rainbow, now there was a bare, butterfly-shaped space on the concrete wall.

The sidewalk was crowded now with office workers on lunch break. I was pulled into the flow so I walked along, dazed. Three blocks from my office, I stopped at the burrito cart that I often frequented on my lunch breaks. They were well-known for their simple but tasty bean-and-rice burritos with really hot salsa. It was so hot, in fact, that for a few minutes I couldn't think about the butterfly as I searched desperately for a cup of water to cool the fire in my throat. After I finished eating, I stayed seated on the bench and tried to make sense of the butterfly, the frog, and the couple with the umbrellas. Was I hallucinating? Had these visions just been a trick of the light; a failure of my eyes; the effects of sleep deprivation, or toxic fumes; or maybe even food poisoning?

The lunch break was ending and I had reached no conclusions. I started my walk back the same way I'd come, intending to take another glance at the butterfly mural. At the last minute, I remembered that there was another mural nearby, so I took a detour.

Almost half a block away, the jazz music began to play. The other passersby must have assumed the saxophone music was merely drifting out of a nearby building. But I knew better. About six months ago, the side of the hardware store on the corner had been painted with a mural. I knew it well: the artist had used mostly browns, yellows and oranges to create a man with an oversized head. It ballooned up to double the proportionate size of his body. The oversized man had his eyes closed as he concentrated on playing a very large saxophone.

My heart beating rapidly, I walked from one end of the mural to the other and then back once more. There was no denying that the music was loudest right in front of the saxophone. I put my face right next to the saxophone. My ear drums rang to the beat of the music. I waited, but the man with the saxophone did not hop off the wall and onto my nose. I kept my face there anyway in case something might happen, until I heard two teenage girls giggling behind me. I am sure they found it strange to see a middle-aged man with his face pressed up against a mural.

Slightly embarrassed, I stepped back from the wall and continued my walk back to the office. Before I went into my building, I crossed the street to look once again at the butterfly mural. The shape of the missing butterfly was still there. No one else seemed to find this remarkable.

By the time I got back to my desk, I was 20 minutes late, but my boss didn't notice. She wouldn't have said anything if she had, given my long-term employment at the company. My co-workers scribbled away in their cubicles, whittling down their mounds of paperwork, but my work for the day was forgotten. My mind was far away from the office. The frog, the couple, the butterfly, the jazz singer—I contemplated each in turn as I stared out my window.

I happened to have a very good view of the mural where the now-missing butterfly had so recently come to life. Although I could not see the finer details, such as the patterns in the other butterflies' wings, I could still see well enough to make out the rainbow, the musical notes, the unpainted butterfly space and the bright flowers.

If I hadn't been staring out the window I certainly would have missed what happened next: a large blue flower in the center of the mural slid off the wall and onto the sidewalk. For no apparent reason at all, it suddenly started to spin clockwise, its petals flapping to and fro. Then it popped up off the ground, and stood upright on its stalk.

The street was eerily empty; I could not see a soul in either direction, and there were no cars, either, which was unusual in the middle of the city in the middle of a weekday. I rubbed my eyes to make sure I wasn't seeing things. The blue flower really had left its two-dimensional world and entered our three-dimensional one. A flower-shaped shadow stretched beneath it on the sidewalk. It was not a small flower; it took up nearly a whole slab of the sidewalk.

I stared, open-mouthed in amazement, as the rainbow followed the flower, making its escape from the wall in the blink of an eye. Red, orange, yellow, green, indigo, blue and violet lines of color moved out of its concrete cage and flowed down the sidewalk. As it started to snake around, rain suddenly fell out of the sky, although there was not a cloud above. Then the black, curvy musical notes danced off the wall, floating one after the other into the sky like helium balloons. They rose up closer and closer to my window on the fourth floor. I opened the window. Rain came in and splattered the papers on my desk, but I didn't care. I could hear the music.

Bling bling bling bling bling. Bloo bloo bloo bloo bloo. Dee dee dee dee dee.

Each of the floating notes had its own unique sound, which flowed perfectly with the other notes. I stuck my head out the window to hear it better, not caring that my hair was getting soaked with rain. An electronic symphony serenaded me as the other two butterflies fluttered out of the mural. They flew up into the air much faster than the musical notes. The pink butterfly stopped and floated right in front of my face for a moment, and then it took off after its companions.

While I'd been watching the butterfly, the rest of the painted flowers had also made their escape. They twirled on the sidewalk—first one way and then the other—to the beat of the still-playing symphony. I couldn't take it anymore. I leapt out of my chair and ran down the stairs. But by the time I stumbled outside, the flowers were all gone. The rain had stopped, too. The only signs of the mural's escape were the puddles on the ground and a blank, concrete wall. I looked up into the sky and there was a long rainbow—longer than any I had ever seen—stretching across the sky. It was brighter than a normal rainbow—so bright I had to shield my eyes from the blinding colors. I wondered if I was seeing an actual rainbow until I noticed that its colors were not in the correct order. Indigo and blue were reversed, just as they had been in the mural.

I waited until the colors faded and the rainbow vanished, as rainbows do, and then I walked back up the stairs. I went into my boss's office and told her that I was not feeling well. It wasn't untrue—my not feeling well. Anyone who watches a mural come to life and dance away is going to feel a bit queasy and perhaps a little motion sick as well. My boss was very understanding, although I didn't tell her the reason I was unwell. She commented on the pale color of my face and suggested I go home early.

I walked quickly to my bus stop, making sure to avoid any known murals. The truth was I could not take any more—at least not yet. I found an empty seat on the bus and opened my book, intending to read. Instead, I just stared at the words, unable to comprehend them. My heart started pounding as we approached the mural of the couple with umbrellas, but when I looked up they were gone. Maybe they had floated off into the air, a gust of wind catching under their umbrellas and carrying them away. Or maybe they were simply walking down the street somewhere pretending to be a normal couple. I looked around the bus half-expecting to recognize the couple as two of my fellow passengers, but I saw only high school kids and tired old men.

When we finally reached my bus stop, I felt even more

nauseous and slightly light-headed. As the bus rumbled away, I glanced at the spot where the frog had been flattened by the semi. There was no sign of the frog's remains, but a streak of lime-green paint stood out luminously against the dark pavement. I could not help but be surprised that there were no people gathered around wondering where it came from or how it got there, or speculating about what it was.

I walked across the street to my house. I needed to lay down for a bit. The house was completely quiet. My wife was at her women's self-empowerment class; I was all alone. I walked straight into my room and climbed into bed fully dressed. I pulled the blankets over my head to block out the sun. I couldn't sleep, but I felt better knowing that I couldn't see any murals, or anything at all.

An hour or so later, my wife came home. I crawled out of bed.

"What are you doing here?" she greeted me. "Your clothes are all wrinkled. Shouldn't you still be at work?"

"Did you see the bright green streak of paint on the road?" I asked her with some urgency.

"Of course I saw it. It sticks out like an overripe pear in a bin of red apples." My wife has a knack for making up fruit-based similes. It's one of the reasons I fell for her in the first place.

"How do you think it got there?"

"Does it matter?" she asked me with a shrug. "I'm sure the city will come and paint over it soon enough. Are you feeling all right?"

I nodded. "I think I just need to get some air."

"At least change your clothes before you go outside."

I ignored my wife's suggestion and walked straight out

the front door in my wrinkled dress shirt and khaki slacks, striped tie hanging loosely around my neck.

I knew exactly where I wanted to go. Although I was a fan of all the murals around town, I did have my favorite, and it was 12 blocks from my house. That was where I was headed, and I knew that I would have to pass a few other murals along the way.

On the corner of my street was a yarn store. For as long as I'd lived there, the building had a mural of kittens playing with a ball of yarn. It had been painted by the store owner, who never had any professional art training so the bodies of the kittens were slightly disproportional. As I walked by, they frolicked about on the sidewalk, not seeming to care that their heads were slightly too big for their bodies and their noses were slightly too small for their whiskers. I stooped down to pet their grey and white fur before continuing on my way.

The sun was shining above and there was no evidence of rainbows or rain puddles or oversized butterflies. In front of the neighborhood music store, a band played enthusiastically. The yellow, green, purple and blue band members played their instruments with complete abandon, but only I stopped to watch. They almost could have passed for regular people who had painted their skin for the occasion of their sidewalk show, but I knew better. Two dancers with gold-colored skin, in slinky red dresses, danced along to the energetic swing music. When I turned to watch them, one of the dancers beckoned me to join her. I obliged. I was grateful my wife had made me take swing lessons with her the year before. The dancer and I twirled and swung all over the parking lot. The artwork band was impressed with our dancing and played with even more vigor. As they played faster and faster, black musical notes appeared on the blank concrete wall behind them.

I stopped when I needed to catch my breath, then bid the golden dancer farewell with a low bow. She curtsied in return and waved goodbye as I disappeared around the corner.

I approached the next mural with some trepidation. The four wolves on the side of the nightclub had always looked ferociously at the disco ball above them. But, no; three simply wagged their tails at me as I walked by, while the fourth one chewed on the disco ball. Other people walked along the street as if nothing out of the ordinary was happening—as if murals always came to life. Maybe they did. Maybe I was the only one who had never noticed before.

I turned the corner, my destination just ahead, when I was suddenly engulfed in a whirlwind of color. Violet, turquoise, navy blue, olive and amber swirled around me. The colors climbed up my legs and ran over my arms. I looked down. My dress shirt was no longer white; now it was a bright shade of purple like the butterfly that had earlier landed on my nose. My pants were now royal blue and gold—as gold as the dancer I had danced with just minutes ago. My tie was every color of the rainbow that had disappeared into the sky.

I was no longer an ordinary man, no longer a boring office worker, no longer a commonplace husband. I was art, made of color and imagination just like the murals. In front of me was exactly what I had been looking for: a hot air balloon, almost as colorful as I now was, with a straw basket hanging down to touch the sidewalk. The door to the basket swung open and a man in a pure white suit beckoned me to join him.

I didn't hesitate. I stepped right in and closed the door behind me. Using a can of white paint and a brush, the man in the white suit sliced the ropes that bound us to the ground. The balloon began to rise.

All my life I'd wanted to ride in a hot air balloon, but I had always been afraid. The day the murals came to life, I was filled with wonder and forgot about the fear. We floated along above the Earth for hours, for days, for weeks. I never felt tired or hungry. I stared down at the world below me and watched as murals around the planet came to life. Music drifted up to us from every corner of the globe. Animals, real and imagined, patterned in every color, raced down sidewalks and across schoolyards and through abandoned lots. Pulsing beats of color flapped and floated and streaked in the air around us. The world was its own mural and I was a part of it.

It may have been months or even years before we touched back down. My wife had been so absorbed with her independence that she had not even noticed my departure, though she greeted me quite warmly. As for myself, I was a changed man. I never did return to my office job or wear a suit and tie again. Instead, I enrolled in art school and learned to paint my own murals.

The original murals never did come back, and the city was so dull with only blank concrete walls. But now I'm the artist. Every day, I paint my city with extravagant colors and look forward to the moment when I will watch my own murals come to life.

The House Guest

"**M**r. Hart just called," my receptionist announced, leaning in my office doorway one Tuesday.

"Did he say why?"

Mr. Hart is one of our biggest clients. I wasn't expecting to hear from him for a few more weeks. I thought happily of the thousands of cartons of Machismo Cigarillos he might be calling to order.

"He wants to borrow your daughter, Mr. Davis."

I picked up the phone.

"I'm throwing a dinner party this Friday night," Mr. Hart explained on the other end of the line. "The mayor will be coming. He was very clear that he wanted my whole family to be there. And well, Charissa, um, won't be able to make it."

His request suddenly made perfect sense. Mr. Hart had a daughter the same age as my own, but with none of the charm of my child. It was well-known in our circle that Charissa had been causing a lot of problems lately, running around with unsavory boys and dying her hair pink. Of course I understood immediately why Mr. Hart would not want the mayor meeting his rebellious daughter. Frankly, if it had been my daughter acting that way I would have sent her to boarding school long ago.

My daughter is my pride and joy. It's amazing how, at 17, she already greatly resembles my wife: delicate features, long auburn hair and bright blue eyes. She has my brains, though; she earns straight A's every semester. She never comes home late and knows not to put her elbows on the dinner table. She is a model child, and I could certainly understand why

Mr. Hart would want to borrow my daughter for his important dinner with the mayor.

That night at home I approached the subject lightly. My daughter is very intelligent and understood right away why it would be advantageous for my business, and therefore our family, if she agreed to pretend to be Mr. Hart's daughter for the night. She was even quite pleased at the prospect of meeting the mayor.

Friday came sooner than expected. My daughter looked just the part of a model child as she twirled happily in her bright yellow sundress, making my wife and I laugh with delight. Before she left, she kissed me on the cheek and told us not to wait up; there would most likely be tea and conversation following the dinner.

Shortly after my daughter left, my wife finished preparing our dinner. It was tomato-basil vermicelli. It was surely not as fancy as what my daughter was being served at Mr. Hart's dinner party for the mayor, but my wife makes a mean pasta sauce. We were just about to sit down to eat when we heard the front door open.

"Who could it be?" my wife mouthed soundlessly to me.

The thought of robbers filled my mind. I stepped in front of my wife and motioned her to be quiet while I picked up a broom to use as a weapon. We froze as we heard a loud thumping noise approaching the kitchen.

Slowly, the kitchen door opened. I could feel my wife shaking with fear behind me. I almost screamed when I saw what came through the door.

Two brown, pointy ears stuck out from the top of a small head that was dominated by an elongated snout. Two large, black eyes barely glanced at us as it hopped into the kitchen on two thick legs. I gaped, and I'm sure my wife was doing the same. It held its short arms out in front. There was a long, fat tail jutting from its bottom. *Thump, thump.* It hopped right past us and plopped down in my daughter's seat at the kitchen table.

The kangaroo made itself right at home. I kept staring, amazed at the skill in its long fingers when it picked up the silver serving spoon and helped itself to a serving of pasta. It placed a decent portion on the plate and then it picked up the fork in one hand and the knife in the other.

Oddly, it didn't start eating. Instead, the kangaroo turned its black eyes to look directly at us, silverware still in hand. I was nervous until I registered the fact that there was nothing malicious in its gaze. In fact, I quickly realized, it was patiently waiting for us.

I looked over at my wife. Surprisingly, she seemed quite calm. She shrugged her shoulders at me as if to say, "Go with the flow!" and took her seat diagonally across from the kangaroo. I followed her, sitting across from our new dinner guest. It watched me, big eyes unblinking, as I picked up the serving spoon and dished myself out a portion and then did the same for my wife. I helped myself to a piece of warm bread from the basket. The kangaroo's eyes turned with interest toward the bread so I broke off a piece for my wife and then another for the kangaroo. I cautiously placed it on its plate, but the kangaroo made no startled movements.

I picked up my fork and knife and began to eat. Only then did the kangaroo begin its meal as well. It ate just like my daughter, taking small bites and being mindful not to put its elbows on the table. Every so often, it would look up from its meal and gaze at us to see if we were enjoying our meal as well. We smiled and nodded our heads reassuringly and the kangaroo went back to eating.

After dinner, the kangaroo hopped up and began to clear the table. It picked up the white plates and silverware and carried them to the sink, and my wife got busy washing them. It had difficulty with the water jug and ended up using its long snout to help balance it. My wife grimaced, but took the jug from the kangaroo anyway before it hopped off to clear the rest of the table.

After the table was clean, it made its way into the living room. Normally, my wife, daughter and I liked to sit together in there after dinner. My daughter would do her homework or read a book, my wife would knit and I would work on the daily crossword puzzle.

My wife and I stayed in the kitchen after the kangaroo went through the door. We stared at each other for a full minute without saying a word.

Finally, my wife whispered, "There's a kangaroo…right? I'm not going crazy, am I?"

"No," I assured her, "I see it too."

We looked helplessly at each other until the kitchen door was once again pushed open. A brown snout and big black eyes peered at us silently, a question in its gaze. I knew it was waiting for us. My wife squeezed my hand once for either courage or support and then we both followed the kangaroo into the living room.

It perched comfortably on my daughter's armchair, *A Tale of Two Cities* propped open beside it. Its eyes focused intently on the page. Every so often it would use the tip of its snout to turn to the next page. A kangaroo reading—well, I had never imagined the likes of it before. I didn't know what else to do so I sat down on the sofa as usual and picked up my crossword puzzle. I confess: I failed to make much progress that night. After an hour of reading, the kangaroo stood and placed its book gently back on the shelf and then hopped out of the room without a backward look at us.

I heard it thumping up the stairs and then down the hallway to my daughter's room. A door opened. Shortly after, a door closed.

Neither my wife nor I slept very well that night. We considered calling the zoo, but the zoo was closed at that hour. We knew better than to call the police. They would have thought we were crazy. Instead, we called our daughter. She didn't pick up, so we left her a voicemail warning her that there was a kangaroo in her room.

When morning came, I told myself it must have been a dream. After all, kangaroos don't simply show up uninvited for dinner at strangers' homes. I came into the kitchen and my hope that it had all been a dream instantly evaporated. The kangaroo was helping my wife make breakfast. It vigorously stirred the pancake mix, concentrating so hard that it didn't turn around when I walked in. My wife seemed quite relaxed for someone cooking breakfast with a kangaroo. I stared for at least a minute before I sat down at the table. I picked up the newspaper, because what else was I to do? It has always been my custom on Saturday mornings.

The pancakes were just as good as usual. They even had blueberries. My wife said it was the kangaroo's idea. I had trouble enjoying them, though, because my daughter still hadn't come downstairs. I went up to look for her in the guest room, but the bed there hadn't been slept in. I checked her room, but she wasn't there, either. I did notice that the kangaroo had made the bed quite tidily.

My daughter definitely wasn't in the house, and she hadn't called us or left a message. I dialed her number again, but it went right to voicemail. I called back a second time because something felt wrong. I realized her voicemail message had changed since the night before. Instead of my daughter's voice kindly asking people to leave a message for Stephanie Davis, I was asked to leave a message for Stephanie Hart. I hung up without leaving a message for anyone.

After breakfast, the kangaroo thumped upstairs and down the hallway again. A door closed. I heard the sound of the shower. While the kangaroo was in the bathroom, I tried to talk to my wife about the latest developments with our daughter.

"Why don't you just leave well enough alone?" she said to me, annoyed. This was not my wife. She had always been a worrywart when it came to our Stephanie. But now she said, "I'm sure she's fine."

"But... there's a kangaroo in our house!"

"She's a very nice kangaroo, dear."

"She?"

"Well, obviously."

This was the end of our conversation or any conversations we would have about our daughter or the kangaroo. Every time I tried to bring it up, my wife would simply change the subject—start talking about the neighbors, ask about my job or talk about the price of tomatoes.

Later that day, we went grocery shopping. The kangaroo came, too. She seemed to like grocery shopping, picking out the same items that my daughter generally chose. None of the other customers or the store clerks commented on the kangaroo's presence despite the thumping noise she made as she hopped down the aisles. I kept expecting to be thrown out for bringing a kangaroo to the supermarket, but nothing like that happened. In fact, no one gave us a second look. Everyone seemed to accept that the kangaroo was a part of our family.

A few days later, we went to the mall—the kangaroo, my wife and I. My wife needed a new pair of tights and the kangaroo seemed to enjoy looking at purses. I wandered out of one the designer handbag stores while the kangaroo was trying on a green, reptilian-looking shoulder bag. Overwhelmed by a feeling of hunger, I was heading over to the pretzel stand when I saw my daughter, Stephanie, walking into the bookstore with Mr. Hart and his wife. My heart sped up and I followed them, keeping back so they wouldn't see me.

I waited until my daughter wandered away from the couple before I approached her.

"Stephanie!" I said urgently. She turned around, giving me a quizzical look. "What's going on? You never came home, and now there's a kangaroo living in our house!"

"I'm sorry," Stephanie said kindly. "Do I know you?"

"Stephanie, it's me—your father!" She looked confused.

"My father is right over there," she said, pointing to Mr. Hart. She still looked just like my wife, but she didn't recognize me. She had no memories of all those times we'd spent together playing catch, raking leaves, having brunch at the diner. It hit me then: Stephanie wasn't my daughter anymore. My daughter was gone. I had lost her the day that I permitted her to be borrowed by Mr. Hart.

"I'm sorry," I mumbled. Then I hurried out of the store.

My life still follows its normal routine. I go to work. I come home. I eat dinner with my family. My wife quickly adjusted to the presence of the kangaroo. She acts as if the kangaroo has always been there. It goes to school, it eats dinner, and it does its homework in the living room. It's as if nothing has changed.

I'm beginning to wonder if maybe it's always been this way. Maybe there's always been a kangaroo staring at me from across the dinner table, waiting patiently for me to come home from work and helping my wife make pancakes. Maybe Stephanie, the daughter I remember, was a figment of my imagination.

A few weeks ago, I had a business meeting with Mr. Hart. I casually inquired about his daughter.

"Stephanie is wonderful," he told me proudly. "In fact, she got along so well with the mayor that she's doing an internship in his office this summer. Isn't that incredible?"

"It is incredible," I agreed. "It is definitely incredible."

Intentions

John Franklin was 28 years old. He is dead. While traveling by train to visit his in-laws, he fell off the platform. He was walking from the dining car to the seating car with his wife when his feet slipped. He was run over by 16 sets of wheels as the train continued to roar down the tracks. His body now resembles a fine, red, papier-mâché explosion. He is survived by his loving wife.

John Franklin was 34 years old. He is dead. While enjoying a home-cooked meatloaf made by his wife, his heart suddenly stopped. He fell forward in his chair, his brown hair quickly soaking up the red merlot that spilled when his upper body prostrated itself across the kitchen table. His pale face smashed a fine china plate the color of a cloud on a warm summer's day. He is survived by his loving wife.

John Franklin was 47 years old. He is dead. While visiting the zoo with his wife, a lion broke through the cage and set upon him, devouring his flesh and crunching on his bones. The lion's motives are unknown. Seven shocked bystanders watched as Franklin's left arm was separated from his torso in one bite. John Franklin died from blood loss before the lion had even begun to lick its lips. He is survived by his loving wife.

John Franklin was 53 years old. He is dead. While hanging Christmas lights on his front porch roof, a sudden wind shook the metal ladder on which he was standing and threw him to the pavement 20 feet below. His skull split open and from it leaked a slow stream of blood, staining the concrete. Broken pieces of red and green glass bulbs were strewn around his corpse. Franklin's wife had requested he hang the lights for all the neighbors to enjoy. He is survived by his loving wife.

John Franklin was 59 years old. He is dead. While coming home from work he was shot in the heart by an unknown assailant who was overflowing with murderous intention. A bouquet of red roses grasped in John's arms floated briefly in the air before striking the pavement. The roses were intended as a gift for his wife. The shooter struck on the victim's 31st wedding anniversary. Franklin died before he met the ground. He is survived by his loving wife.

John Franklin was 64 years old. He is dead. While plugging in the television for his wife on Tuesday morning, he experienced a brutal electric shock. The savage jolt initiated its deadly path in the tips of John's fingers and quickly spread throughout his body. This caused an abrupt cessation of heartbeat and Franklin's body concluded its function. He is survived by his loving wife.

Mary Franklin is 78 years old. She is alive. She has plotted the death of her husband at least six times during the course of their marriage. Fifty years ago, she bought herself a train ticket to go visit her family by herself. When her husband surprised her by buying a ticket to accompany her, she'd tried to push him off the platform of the train by pretending to stumble into him. He quickly recovered and insisted on taking her arm and helping her walk to the next car.

Six years later, John had surprised Mary by coming home early while she was packing her bags to leave him for good. That evening, she cooked rat poison into his meatloaf. But John had a sour stomach that day and wasn't hungry. Not wanting to hurt his wife's feelings, he secretly fed his portion to the dog. No one investigated the dog's sudden death.

When Mary and John were in their forties, John spent their life savings on a hot tub for the backyard. Mary had been planning to use that money for a one-way trip to California, alone. Later that week, Mary sprayed the inside of one of his shirts with bacon grease and surprised him with a trip to the zoo. She knew her husband had a compromised sense of smell, but the lion couldn't resist the aroma and managed to break out of its cage. But the animal, born and raised in captivity, lacked the necessary killer instinct. It proceeded to give John the bath of his lifetime as he giggled happily.

A few years later, Mary brightly suggested her husband put up the Christmas lights even though December was still a month away. After he climbed the ladder, Mary stopped watering the gardenias and walked over to his ladder, grabbed the bottom rungs and vigorously shook it. John looked down to see her steadying the ladder after a harsh gust of wind, and he waved his thanks as he finished stringing the last of the lights.

Nearing her sixties and tired of trying to leave, Mary hid behind her neighbors' hydrangea with a shotgun. When her husband appeared she pulled the trigger, aiming for his heart. She missed and grazed his ear instead. When he suddenly started bleeding, he thought a low-hanging, sharp tree branch was the culprit. John apologized profusely for spoiling their celebration as his wife drove him to the hospital on their anniversary.

Her last attempt on his life occurred 14 years ago. She stripped the electrical cords of the unplugged television and then asked her husband to please plug it in. Expecting a shock to hit her husband, she was disappointed when he merely received a light tingling feeling in his fingertips, which he called "refreshing."

Mary Franklin is 79. She is dead. She died from natural causes. Her body was placed in a casket and lowered solemnly into the ground. Her friends and family sat by and wept. She is survived by her loving husband.

John Franklin is 80. He is dead. He died from a broken heart not two months after his wife's passing. Shortly before his death, he told his friends that his life had lost its meaning when she died. His body has been placed inside a casket and lowered down beside her, where they will be together for eternity, just as he always wanted.

The Heart Balloon

I never thought that I would wear my heart on my sleeve, let alone in a balloon, where everyone could see it.

It was love's fault that my heart turned into this—the bastard.

It all started on a Saturday in the middle of June. My friends organized a trip to the beach. I'd been working on my six pack all spring, so I was ready.

The beach is only five or six miles from my house. I packed all the essentials: sunscreen, a towel and beer. The sun was out and already heating up the city when I left my house. It was the perfect day to catch a cool ocean breeze.

It was Saturday, so the beach was brimming with families. Mothers in one-piece suits sunbathed while their husbands—noses and bald spots covered in white sunscreen—bounced young babies on their knees. Small children ran across the sand, their high-pitched voices ringing in the air.

After we dumped our stuff by the dunes, I ran straight into the water, drenching myself and splashing hand-made waves at my buddies. Eventually, we were ready to take a break from the water and enjoy the beach's warm sand. After the third sand castle had collapsed and the fourth beer had been drunk, it was time for lunch. My friend Sandy, who has always been the prepared type, pulled out a picnic basket she'd hauled down the beach and unpacked an elaborate picnic lunch. We were laughing and chowing down on peanut butter and jelly sandwiches dusted with beach sand when I saw her.

She was wearing a yellow and pink striped dress, which looked like a uniform of some kind. Her dark brown hair was cut short and her pink lips were turned up in a smile as she handed a small boy a bright red balloon.

Up until that exact moment I'd always been happily single. Casual dating had been my thing and I was a real pro at it. But seeing her, I changed. I was, as my favorite hip-hop artists say, "sprung."

She was not just cute or pretty; she was stunning. I had to buy a balloon.

I dropped the uneaten half of my sandwich in the sand and dug my wallet out of my backpack. I had no idea how much a balloon cost. I grabbed all the cash from my wallet, just in case, and ran to catch up to her. She was making her way down the beach, balloons bobbing along in tow.

"And what color balloon would you like, sir?" she asked me in the most perfect, joyful voice that I have ever heard.

I froze up. I hadn't been expecting such a difficult question. If I picked black or blue she might think me too rough. If I picked pink or purple she might think I was gay or that I was buying a balloon to give to my girlfriend.

"Green," I finally blurted out, unsure if I'd made the right decision.

"That'll be 50 cents."

I gave her a dollar bill, painfully aware that my hand was shaking. She calmly took the money and our hands just barely grazed. She effortlessly made change and handed me my balloon.

"Have a good day, sir" she said, ending our conversation far too quickly.

My hand flowed with a warm tingle where hers had brushed it. I grasped the balloon tightly and walked away. It had all happened too quickly; I'd lost my chance.

When I returned to my friends they laughed at me and my green balloon, but I didn't pay them much attention. My thoughts were on the balloon girl. I wondered if I should chase after her and buy a second balloon so we could talk again. But that might seem too desperate. My friends didn't pick up on my inner turmoil, but they were enjoying teasing me about how I'd tied the balloon around my wrist as soon as I sat down. I knew how it looked, but I didn't care at that point. I had to be careful with the balloon; after all, the balloon girl gave it to me. I needed to make sure it wouldn't fly away.

By the time I decided I would make a second attempt, the balloon girl was nowhere in sight. My friends and I stayed at the beach until sunset and I kept looking for her, but she didn't come back. When the sun went down, I went home with the balloon still tied tightly around my wrist. I vowed to myself that I would find the balloon girl again.

She was all I could think about. So early the following day, I packed my lunch, a couple of cold beverages (for the nerves), sunscreen and plenty of dollar bills for balloons.

I found a place on the beach right near where my friends and I had sat the day before. I looked to the left and to the right but I didn't see the balloon girl. After an hour or so, I jumped into the ocean for a bit, to pass the time. I didn't go in very far. I made sure to stay within sight of the area of the beach where the balloon girl had appeared the day before. After a little while I got out of the water, dried off, drank a beer and then slowly ate a sandwich.

Finally, after what felt like a whole day, she appeared. I pulled a dollar bill out of my wallet and ran over to her.

"Hi," I said, breathing heavily from the sprint. Adrenaline

was pumping through me just from being close to her again.

"Hello," she replied calmly. "What color balloon would you like?"

"Yellow," I answered confidently. I'd thought about it all night. Yellow is a calm, nurturing color—the perfect color to choose for impressing the balloon girl.

Once again money was exchanged and our hands brushed. She handed me the string to a yellow balloon and two quarters in change. I accepted the balloon and the change and she turned away and headed down the beach. I turned to follow her, but stopped as I realized my mind had gone blank. I had nothing to say so I walked away dejectedly.

I watched her sell balloons down the beach and when I could no longer see her on the horizon I walked back to my car and drove home, a failure. I needed a better plan.

The next morning, a Monday, I didn't have classes because I was on summer break. I rose early and packed for the beach. Lying in bed the night before, I'd come up with a plan. The balloon girl always showed up around lunch time, so it was possible she would be feeling hungry around the time she came by my part of the beach. Instead of packing my usual two sandwiches, I packed four. It had taken me an hour or two to decide what kind of sandwiches to make. I didn't know if the balloon girl was a vegetarian, but just in case she was I couldn't go with deli meat. What if she was allergic to nuts? I couldn't risk peanut butter and jelly. Finally, I decided on avocado and hummus. I made some with lettuce and tomato and some without, just in case.

Even though it was still early, I drove over to the beach and lay my blanket down in the usual spot. I didn't bother going into the water this time or trying to build a sand castle. I sat and waited. I rehearsed what I would say to her and then changed my mind and then changed it again.

When the sun had almost reached its peak she appeared. I grabbed a dollar and a sandwich. Instead of sprinting, I walked purposefully toward her. I had planned it all out; I had this down, I reminded myself. I was going to eat the sandwich while getting the balloon. She'd see how tasty it looked and wouldn't be able to resist when I invited her to join me for one on my blanket. I'd asked girls out before. This shouldn't be hard.

"What color balloon would you like?"

"Nobrano. Whaddya ryke a sandwish?"

I realized my mouth was full of sandwich. I had been so hungry that I had taken a bite without even realizing. I swallowed quickly, feeling my face turn bright red.

She laughed.

I laughed too.

"Umm," I started again, once my mouth was clear. "Would you like a sandwich? No nuts or meat..." I regretted those words the minute I said them.

But she just laughed again. It was loud, but not annoyingly loud. More like happy-loud.

"What I mean is I have hummus, avocado, lettuce, and tomato if you want. I mean, if you're hungry." I made myself shut up.

"Sure," she said, gifting me with a smile. "As a matter of fact, I'm starving!"

I thought for a second that I might pass out from happiness. The hot sun and the three nerve-killing beers I'd already polished off weren't helping, either.

She followed me back to my blanket, dragging her cart

behind her. I offered to help, but she smiled again and said she had it, no problem. Everything was going really well and we'd just made it to my blanket when Sandy showed up.

"Jeff! Hey!" she hollered at me, waving from the dunes by the parking lot.

Damn it, I thought. Sandy has always had the worst timing.

"My friend Sandy," I told the balloon girl awkwardly, adding "not my girlfriend or anything, just a friend." I didn't want her to get the wrong idea.

"Hi!" said Sandy when she reached the blanket. "Who's this?"

"I'm Karen," said the balloon girl.

"Sandy."

"I'm Jeff, by the way," I said, wishing I'd introduced myself earlier.

Sandy dropped down on my blanket uninvited and made herself right at home, helping herself to a sandwich, asking Karen questions about herself and mostly ignoring me. I would have grumbled my annoyance, but I didn't want Karen to see me lose my cool.

As it turned out, Sandy and Karen had a lot in common. They were both vegetarians (I congratulated myself on having that covered in the sandwich making). They both were studying English at the university we all attended. I mentioned that I was studying business, but they'd already moved on to talk about music. It turned out they both had the same favorite band, which was some alternative punk group that I'd never heard of.

All too soon, Karen said she had to return to work. She got up to leave and waved goodbye to the both of us.

"Oh, and Jeff," I could feel my heart beat faster when she

said my name, "thank you so much for lunch. The sandwiches were delicious. Here, let me give you a balloon."

Before I could politely decline (even though I really did want a balloon) she started digging around in her cart.

"What color do you want?"

"Um, any color is good. You choose."

She handed me a red balloon. I was ecstatic. Red is the color of love, after all.

"Bye," she said, pushing her cart away.

I watched her go and then I tied the balloon to my wrist. I looked up at it as it floated in the air above me. I was so happy that I pulled it down and hugged the balloon tightly to my chest, right up against my heart.

In that moment, my heart suddenly felt warmer than I'd ever experienced or could have imagined. As I hugged the balloon, I could feel the beating in my chest speed up, beating faster and faster. And then the balloon started changing. Suddenly, it was no longer an oval balloon shape; it became heart-shaped.

I stared in amazement. And then I realized that I could no longer feel the beating of my own heart anymore. I put my hand against my chest. I felt nothing, not even a light thumping. My chest was still. I put my hand against the balloon. It thumped in a familiar rhythm of my heartbeat. I was so surprised I yelled out loud. My heart had become a balloon.

Sandy was swimming in the water. I quickly packed up my stuff and I called to her that I had to get going.

I drove right home and went directly inside. I paced back and forth, unsure of what to do with my heart. I tried hugging the balloon again to force my heart back into my chest—being careful not to hug it too hard lest it pop. But nothing changed. The balloon stayed a heart and my chest remained empty.

Eventually, overwhelmed with fear, I started to cry. I cried all night and then I cried myself to sleep, the balloon still attached to my wrist.

I woke up on Tuesday to the sound of the phone ringing. It was Sandy asking if I wanted to meet at the beach again. I told her no, I was feeling ill, and hung up the phone.

I thought briefly of the balloon girl, but I didn't want to leave the house for fear of my heart accidentally popping. I didn't dare leave it unattended at home, either, where the cat could shred it.

I sat down at my laptop and started to Google. I searched every search engine, even the ones I had never heard of before that day. I even posted on a couple of surreal experience forums, but I couldn't find a single reference to hearts being turned into balloons—or, more importantly, how to reverse the process.

I spent a day and a night on the computer and finally gave up. I was left with only one option: I had to give my heart to Karen. That was my only hope. After all, she was the balloon girl.

I went to bed. I was exhausted from searching and quickly fell asleep.

The alarm woke me early and I left my house soon after. I headed straight to the beach. But instead of sitting on the sand, I stayed in my car, in the parking area above the dunes. I'd brought binoculars and I focused them on the stream of people walking down the beach. Karen would be easy to pick out.

The weather was perfect, but I sat in my car protecting

my heart all morning. I'd gotten there early, just in case, but it was once again around noon when I saw her pushing her cart up the beach. She was as lovely as before.

I noticed Sandy was with her. I wasn't that surprised. I knew Sandy had planned on coming to the beach today. I imagined they were talking about their favorite band, maybe books, too; maybe even boys. I cringed at the thought of all the embarrassing things Sandy could be telling Karen about me right now.

Before leaving my car, I untied the balloon string from my wrist. I gripped it tightly in my hand and took in a deep breath. Then I walked across the sand to intercept her.

"Karen!" I called out, moving toward her, my feet sinking into the sand.

She turned around. "Oh, hey, Jeff." She was pushing her cart with one hand. I stopped right in front of her.

"I want to give you this." I held the balloon out to her. It floated right in front her, but she didn't touch it. Then I looked down and I saw why. Her free hand was occupied. She was holding hands with Sandy.

I gasped and accidentally let go of the balloon.

I tried to jump and grab it, but it was too fast for me. It floated up and up and then it was gone.

Sandy laughed. Karen tried to apologize. Neither of them understood the gravity of the situation. I could feel tears start to well in my eyes. My heart was gone. I turned away and ran back to my car.

So here I am, a heartless man. I don't know where it is now. Perhaps it has gotten stuck in a cloud. Perhaps a seagull has swallowed it whole, or perhaps it is floating around in the stratosphere somewhere, looking for love, while down on the ground I'm left to worry and wonder about my missing heart.

Mary –
The Interesting Girl

Mary was always a pretty girl. Not stunning, not gorgeous, but pretty. She was taller than most girls, but not so tall that she had to wear flat shoes to dance with the men she met at the nearby bar on Friday nights. Mary didn't dye her long hair; she liked the brown color she was born with. She didn't have to tweeze her eyebrows very much, either. They naturally grew in two, almost-perfect arcs. Makeup was a chore Mary didn't spend too much time on. A light shade of pink lipstick usually sufficed for day-to-day events.

Mary was ordinary enough, at least according to her friends and the baristas at her favorite coffee shop and the people she chatted with on the number 12 bus when she took it downtown to the architecture firm where she worked as a receptionist. They all thought she was ordinary, at least until the day she did something quite extraordinary.

The day that Mary failed to show up for work was a regular Tuesday. It wasn't Election Day or Veteran's Day. It was just a normal Tuesday, and Mary wasn't the type of girl who simply didn't show up for work. Her manager didn't know what to think. Mary didn't show up the next day, either, or the day after that. After a few missed days of work, Mary's co-workers started to worry. They phoned her family, but none of them had heard from Mary, nor had any of her friends. Mary had simply disappeared.

"Ordinary girls don't just disappear," her friends said. "No one can suddenly stop being ordinary."

Mary's family worried. She'd never gone off by herself

without telling someone before. That was not the type of girl Mary was. She had always been quite considerate and had never been in any trouble.

Mary had no boyfriend. Someone suggested that maybe she'd met a man and run away with him. But the people who knew Mary had trouble believing it. Mary was not the type of girl to run away with a fellow.

A search party was formed. Perhaps she'd drowned, some people speculated. The police dredged the rivers, but they found nothing but old tires. Mary's friends weren't surprised. She had always been a very good swimmer. They had tried to tell the police.

The morgue was checked. Could she have been hit by a car and become so disfigured that she was now quite unrecognizable? Feet with missing toes were thoroughly scrutinized, and eyes that could no longer see were examined in depth. It was scientifically determined that none of them belonged to Mary.

Kidnapped? Burned alive? Captured by gypsies? Theories continued to pop up, each one more and more extravagant. Not a day went by when someone didn't declare that Mary had joined a cult and had quickly been promoted to the leader due to her hard work, or that Mary had run off with the circus and was now a lion tamer, or something of the sort. A year passed like this, until the day that Mary returned.

It was 9 a.m. on a Tuesday, and Mary walked into work. She was wearing her brown skirt and sensible shoes, with a light coating of pink lipstick—same as usual. The architecture firm had long since hired someone new to replace Mary, but when she walked through the door, management hired her back on the spot. After all, how could they lose an employee as interesting as Mary?

The girl who had replaced Mary was moved to a new department. She had been quite a good receptionist for the firm—more welcoming and friendlier than Mary had been, not that Mary had ever been cold or rude. This girl just had a more outgoing personality and people immediately liked her. But Mary was a legend now in the community. A savvy manager knew that having her at the front desk would only attract more attention for their company.

They were quite right. Although there were plenty of more innovative and cost-effective architecture firms in the area, people flocked to Mary's firm just to see the extraordinary girl who had disappeared and then reappeared.

Mary's bosses did not ask her where she'd been. The mystery was enough for them. It was not enough, however, for Mary's friends and family. They asked, they pleaded, they begged Mary to tell them where she had gone. Yet no matter what they said, all Mary would do was smile and look away. Where Mary had spent the previous year was her biggest secret, perhaps her only secret, and she refused to relinquish it.

Although Mary was still pretty much the same girl she'd been before her disappearance, (same brown hair, same arched eyebrows, same pale-pink lipstick) she now had at least three dates a week. All the guys in town wanted to date a girl as interesting as Mary. She had more friends, too. Everyone wanted to get to know the famous Mary. She was a sensible girl, though, and knew not to give up her old friends for her new ones. Her old friends enjoyed the benefits of Mary's popularity.

Mary's parents insisted that she see a doctor. They assumed that wherever she had gone had affected her health in some way. Mary went, and the doctor found nothing wrong with her. Same height, same freckles, same slightly crooked toe. Mary was exactly the same girl she'd been before she disappeared. After her physical, the doctor assured her of doctor-patient confidentiality and eagerly asked Mary where she had gone. Mary simply smiled and kept her mouth shut.

Years passed, and quite a few of the men that Mary dated proposed marriage to her. She took her time deciding; after all, she was in no rush to settle down. Eventually, she chose the son of the town's dentist. He was a well-known and well-liked young man. He was handsome, played quite a few sports and was studying to be a lawyer. All the other young women were jealous of Mary's catch, but they agreed that he and Mary made a suitable couple since they were both so very interesting.

As married couples often do, Mary and her husband had children—two, to be exact: a boy and a girl. A lot of speculation came up about them when they were first born. But they turned out to be quite ordinary, just as Mary once had been.

It was not long after Mary became a parent that she decided to leave her receptionist position. Nobody faulted her for giving up a career in the work world to be a full-time homemaker. After all, she had lived such an interesting life up until then. It made sense that she would want to settle down now.

For quite a while, she was content being an ordinary housewife. Mary's husband was happy as well, since he had such an interesting wife, and Mary's two kids were happy, too, that they had such an interesting mother. The town, as well, was happy to have such an interesting person living among them.

Time passed and, as is inevitable, Mary grew old. The people in town were sad to realize that Mary's interesting life was so close to coming to an end.

On the day when it was clear that she was dying, the mayor of the town went to visit her. He had been a young boy when Mary disappeared, but he remembered quite vividly the excitement and buzz surrounding the mystery of her disappearance. The old woman lay comfortably on her deathbed and greeted him with a tired smile. He drew a chair up to her bedside and paid his respects. He told her that she would be missed, and that he and the town had a final request. Before Mary died, would she please, finally, tell them what had been so interesting that it had taken Mary away from them for an entire year so long ago? Mary nodded, gathering her breath for her final words.

"Why, mayor," she said in a whisper, "I never went anywhere. I guess I just slept too long one night, and the world went on without me."

The Green Patio Chair

"What am I going to do with this chair?" the man asked himself. He examined the bright green piece of patio furniture. He had spotted the Adirondack chair at a yard sale around the corner, and it was on sale for the low price of 50 cents. He couldn't pass up the bargain. He had picked it up and brought it home, only to place it in his garage. What does one do with a bright green patio chair?

He considered his other patio chairs, all a perfectly calm shade of off-white that matched the table that came with the set. The green chair stuck out like a ripe banana on an apple tree. It was different, and maybe that was what had first attracted him.

His wife pulled up in her minivan and started unloading groceries. She took a step back when she saw the chair. He persuaded her to sit down in it, but she stood a second later.

"It's merely an uncomfortable lawn ornament," she declared. "What are you going to do with it?"

"Perhaps I could paint it," the man mumbled. After all, he did still have that can of off-white paint under his workbench. But it seemed like such a shame to paint a chair when it was not chipped or peeling. And even with a few coats of off-white, there was still the matter of the chair's odd scalloped shape, and cutting it up just would not do.

The man took another look at his new chair and said, "That settles it."

He carried the chair around to the back of the house and shuffled the off-white chairs around to make room for it among the rest of the furniture, which glared at it accusingly. Relieved to have found a place for it, the man went inside to pour himself something to drink. He'd always found that making decisions was thirsty work.

Walking through the back door, he glanced back and smiled at the chair. The furniture decorating his yard no longer matched, but something in his life finally had character.

Love at First Sip

It was the heart in her morning soy latte that changed everything. It was a slightly off-sided white puff of foam, shaped mostly like a heart, and complete with little clouds of latte foam forming below it.

And then when he smiled wide, his perfect white teeth showing through pink lips, and said "Have a great day!" Christie knew she was in love.

She had never had a boyfriend. She was not exactly what most people would refer to as pretty or even average looking. When she was a child, people would sometimes refer to her as cute, but as she grew older, people would no longer refer to her as anything at all. Most people didn't even know her name. For the most part, Christie was ignored. They ignored her—with her nappy hair, which stayed that way no matter how many times she brushed it, and uneven ears, which made her glasses sit crookedly on her unfortunate, too-big-for-her-face nose. She was used to being ignored and it had long ago ceased to bother her. That is, until the day he first started working at Christie's usual coffee shop.

Every morning before work Christie walked the two drab blocks from her apartment to the coffee shop and ordered a soy latte to go. The baristas there were highly talented, although lacking in friendliness. With ease, they created foam teardrops or white waves of sadness in her latte. Christie wondered if they pitied her because she was always alone. Perhaps that was why they drew such sad pictures in her coffee. But the baristas probably didn't think about her at all. They never made small talk with her at the register, or even asked her for her name. They simply took her money and returned with a hot soy latte. She spent most of the bus ride to work looking at the picture in the latte and carefully sipping around the foam.

It went on like this for five years: every weekday Christie arrived at the cafe at precisely 8:11 in the morning. She would order her soy latte and be out the door by 8:14. Her routine was unchanging until the day Alex showed up.

It was 8:13 am, and Christie stood silently, arms folded, in the corner nearest to the counter. The new barista was taking longer than usual to finish making her drink and Christie was beginning to worry she might miss the 8:17 bus, which picked her up right around the corner. She was picturing the bus driving away without her at the very moment the new barista placed the latte in front of her.

At first Christie thought that he must have made a mistake. She must have received the wrong latte. This could not possibly be her drink. The foam picture was not sad at all; it was happy. The white had been formed into a heart. It was a little lopsided, but it was definitely a heart.

"Have a great day!" the barista said to her, smiling widely

Christie was in utter shock. She did not drink a single sip of her latte on the way to work. Instead, she stared at the heart in the cup and remembered the smile and the eyes of the boy who had drawn a heart for her and told her to "Have a great day!"

When she got to work, Christie could not concentrate. Her soy latte sat beside her, untouched, as she stared blankly at her computer screen. Every few seconds she would glance back over to the cup. She was irate when she came back from lunch to find that the janitor had thrown the untouched drink away.

The next day, Christie awoke five minutes early so as to give the new barista sufficient time to make her latte.

She was rewarded this time with a beautiful flower. At least, she thought it was a flower. The petals were kind of squished together, but it definitely resembled a flower, she was certain of it. In addition to the flower, Christie received another "Have a great day!" with a genuine smile to go with it.

Once again, Christie left her drink untouched and spent her work day staring into the cup and replaying his words over and over in her memory. She took her untouched drink with her to lunch to save it from the janitor.

She was in love, and it only got worse.

The next day, when Christie arrived at the coffee shop, the new barista was standing behind the register.

"You must be a regular," he said to Christie.

Christie nodded, unable to speak.

"I'm Alex. What's your name?"

"Ch-ch-ch-ristie," she mumbled.

Alex did not even blink at her stammering. "Nice to meet you, Christie," he said cheerfully as he poured a four leaf clover, with an extra leaf, in the center of her soy latte.

That day was Friday. Christie always called her parents on Fridays after she got off work. Normally, she would not say much to her mother, who rambled on and on about the lives of all of Christie's siblings, all of whom were married and had children. Christie's mother never asked Christie any questions about her life. However, this time Christie had something that she wanted to say to her mom.

"Mom," she interrupted when her mother paused to catch her breath during a 10-minute story about how Christie's pregnant sister-in-law could not decide between the names

Adam and Chad if it was a boy. Christie's mom, so surprised that her daughter interrupted her, immediately stopped her story right in the middle.

"Mom, I have a boyfriend."

Silence followed the statement as it sunk in. Then her mother's elated voice shouted "Hallelujah!" She had long since given up on the idea that her youngest daughter would ever find herself a boyfriend.

"What's his name?" she asked.

"Alex"

"What does he do?"

"He's a barista, and an amazing one, too."

Christie's mom pelted her with question after question about his looks, interests and personality. Christie answered each question enthusiastically. She didn't even have to pause to think. Somehow, she just knew the answers.

"Does he love you?" Christie's mom finally asked.

"Well," Christie replied, "he hasn't said so, yet. But he gave me a heart, so I know he does!"

It was the best conversation they'd had since Christie was eight.

Christie did not normally go to her coffee shop on Saturdays, but she didn't think she could wait two whole days to see Alex again, so she set her alarm clock instead of sleeping in and arrived at her coffee shop at precisely 8:06 in the morning.

"Well, good morning Christie," said Alex, as she walked through the door. "How are you today?"

"I'm good."

"That's good. I'm glad, that you're well."

Tongue-tied, Christie could not think of a single thing to say back.

"Do you have to work today?" Alex asked.

Christie could feel the color pool in her cheeks, "Um, no, I have the weekend off."

"Ah," said Alex, "how nice. I wish that I had the day off. Soy latte to go?"

"For here." Christie was amazed to hear herself say that. She had never before ordered her drink "for here" before.

"For here, then," said Alex, smiling at her.

A few minutes later, Alex handed Christie her drink. It was another heart, more symmetrical this time. He was improving. She sat down at a table near the counter. Luckily, she always brought a book with her everywhere she went. She pulled out the book, but didn't even try to read. She merely stared at the black Times New Roman font on the page, occasionally glancing up at Alex. Somehow, every time she looked up she failed to notice that the smile he gave to her was the same he gave to every customer. In her mind, his special smile was for her alone.

She didn't want to drink her latte and ruin the heart, but she knew she couldn't take it with her. So she sipped it as slowly as she possibly could. It wasn't until almost two hours later when she finally finished it and got up to leave.

"Have a great afternoon!" Alex called out to her with a wave.

"You, too," she said, and she rushed out of the shop.

Christie raced straight home. Once in her kitchen, she paced back and forth for hours, reliving the conversation she and Alex had had that morning.

"He loves me," she thought, "he must! And I love him."

The next day, Christie again woke up early in order to see

Alex. But he wasn't there when she walked through the door at 8:06 a.m.

"What do you want?" one of the regular baristas asked with disinterest.

"Where's Alex?" she asked.

"Day off," the barista said, eyeing her suspiciously.

Christie ordered a soy latte to go. She didn't even bother to look at the picture as she broodingly took the cup off the counter and walked out the door. She was angry at Alex for not telling her that he had the day off. She had expected to see him. He'd let her down. She hadn't even thought for a second that he might not be there.

She went home and sat down at her kitchen table, where two soy lattes (the one from Thursday and the one from Friday) sat, still untouched. She stared at the cups. Just seeing them pacified her. She thought about the pictures that Alex had so delicately drawn for her.

Christie forgave Alex. After all, that's what lovers do.

Alex wasn't at the coffee shop on Monday, either. Christie was upset when she got to work with her sad soy latte. But after thinking about it for a while, she understood why Alex had not told her about his two days off. After all, they were still in the beginning stage of their relationship. Christie shouldn't pressure him to tell her his complete schedule—at least not just yet.

The next day, Alex was back behind the counter.

"Good morning, Christie," he greeted her.

"Hi, Alex." She felt bold saying his name aloud.

"How are you today?" He grinned broadly at her as usual, as if he hadn't been gone the past two days.

"Ok… Um, you, you weren't here yesterday." Christie

could feel her cheeks turn bright red.

"That's true. Sundays and Mondays are my days off. Soy latte to go?"

"Yes." Her heart warmed. He understood. He'd told her his schedule!

The days passed and Christie's living room table filled with untouched soy lattes. Her normally clean, fake-lemon-scented apartment now smelled bitter and moldy, although Christie never noticed. Flies gathered around the cups, but Christie didn't care. Nobody else ever came into her apartment, anyway.

Since Alex had told her that he didn't work on Sundays or Mondays, Christie stopped going to the coffee shop on those days. She did not want to have to see even one more sad soy latte—not ever.

On Tuesdays, Wednesdays, Thursdays, Fridays and Saturdays, at 8:06 a.m., Christie found Alex behind the counter at the café. She still blushed when Alex talked to her and was far too nervous to say anything witty back to him. But it didn't matter, at least not in Christie's mind. In Christie's mind, she and Alex had been going steady for almost two months now and things were starting to grow quite serious. She had never felt so alive and excited about her life as she had during the past eight weeks.

Everything was going great until one Saturday. On Saturdays, Christie would always order her coffee "for here." That way, she could sit and surreptitiously watch Alex while she pretended to read her book. She was sitting at her usual table, near the end of the counter where Alex stood. She saw Alex come out from behind the counter and greet a girl wearing black-framed glasses and a yellow plaid shirt. He said something to her that Christie couldn't hear, laughed warmly, and then he kissed her. Alex called to a co-worker that he was taking his break and then he and the girl walked outside together, laughing. Alex didn't even turn to look at her as he left.

Christie was stunned. Her mouth hung open in surprise. Did that really just happen? Alex would never betray her like that—not her Alex! She looked out the window and there he was, walking away with his arm around the girl.

"How could he!" she thought, anger burning in her veins. "It's as if I'm not even here! It's like I'm completely invisible to him!"

Christie quickly got up from her table and left, abandoning her still mostly full drink. Outside, she started to cry. Christie cried the two blocks back to her apartment. She continued to cry as she locked the door behind her and sat down at the table in front of three dozen old soy lattes. She did not stop crying until long after the sun went down and there were no tears left.

The next morning, Christie woke up covered in old soy latte. She'd knocked over a couple of the cups while she slept, having cried herself to sleep at her kitchen table. Seeing the coffee that Alex had given her now in a puddle on the table made her almost start to cry again. But she didn't. Instead, Christie got up and took a shower, washing away the smell of salty tears and old coffee. By the time she stepped out of the shower, she had a fully formed plan. Alex was confused, but it was okay. Christie would show him the truth. Never again would Alex's lips touch another girl's. Never again.

Tuesday morning, Christie would normally be ordering her drink at her coffee shop at 8:06, but she wasn't this morning. No, Christie would be there later. Right now, she was getting ready. She'd called in sick the day before and explained that she would be out for at least two days. She told her boss that she'd come down with the flu. Her boss's only reply was a low grunt of understanding.

Yesterday had found Christie at the hardware store, where she'd purchased supplies: 10 feet of rope, a collapsible ladder, duct tape and a blunt knife (just in case). All of these were now packed in a black backpack at Christie's feet.

Alex got off work at 3 p.m. She knew this, as he had casually mentioned it to her a few weeks ago. She remembered he'd said that he liked getting out of work then because the buses weren't too crowded at that hour.

At 2:45 p.m., Christie left her apartment, backpack hooked over her shoulder. She pretended to look busy as she lingered around the corner across the street from the coffee shop, waiting for Alex to emerge.

At exactly 3 p.m., Alex stepped out the door of the coffee shop. Instead of walking up to the bus stop where Christie was waiting, he held the door open and pulled out a little red wagon. The manager had asked him to go to the supply warehouse to pick up 50 pounds of dark-roast Guatemalan coffee beans. It was not a long walk, maybe half a mile, and the wagon would make it easy for him to transport the beans. Alex enjoyed going to the warehouse. It smelled deliciously of fresh-ground coffee. The company roasted all the beans there and then finely ground them in a giant grinder that was as tall as a basketball player and as wide as a wrestler pumped up on steroids.

Alex wasn't thinking of anything important as he strolled

down the street toward the warehouse. It was a nice day outside, and he idly wondered if his girlfriend, Shelby, might want to go to the park with him to play frisbee. He didn't notice Christie skulking along behind him.

Alex had noticed that the shy girl, Christie, missed her soy latte that morning. Alex was fond enough of Christie. She was always friendly and tipped well. He liked all the regulars at the coffee shop.

Christie stayed half a block behind Alex as he walked. She could not help but wonder why he was dragging a little red wagon along. He actually looked pretty adorable with the wagon in tow.

Finally, Alex stopped in front of a brick warehouse and maneuvered the wagon inside with him. Christie crept up to the metal door, waiting a full minute before slipping inside.

Alex thought he heard a noise. He turned to look, but it was dim inside the warehouse and he didn't see anything. He turned back around and began to load bags of freshly ground coffee into his little red wagon.

Christie froze when Alex turned around. She stood very still until a moment later when he turned his back to her.

Now the rope was in her hands and she tiptoed closer and closer to him. "This is for Alex's own good," she thought, preparing to lunge.

Struggling to keep the bags from slipping off each other, Alex heard footsteps behind him. He turned just as someone threw a rope around him.

Alex was much stronger than Christie, despite his skinny arms. It wasn't until Alex had flung his attacker over the metal railing that enclosed the giant coffee grinder that he recognized her. Christie, whose face was normally a bright, blushing red, now had a face contorted in fear as she flew into the grinder. Alex was so surprised that he took a few steps back, accidentally hitting the "on" switch.

The loud whirring of the coffee grinder completely drowned out the sounds of Christie's screaming. Frantically, he fumbled for the "off" switch, but it was too late. The screaming had stopped.

Alex was horrified. He looked down into the coffee grinder expecting to see a pile of blood, flesh and mangled bones. Instead, there were only black coffee grounds. He blinked a few times and looked again. No Christie; only coffee. His nose filled with the delicious smell of pure, dark, fresh-ground coffee.

The smell was so decadently rich that he completely forgot about where the coffee grounds had come from. He grabbed a small, brown paper bag and scooped the fresh coffee grounds into it.

In the corner of the warehouse there was a tasting area with an electric kettle, an espresso maker, a French press and cups. Alex measured out three tablespoons into the French press and added boiling water from the kettle. He could barely wait the three minutes; it smelled fantastic. When the timer went off, he pushed down the plunger and poured himself a single cup of coffee. The smell was so good that he did not even wait for it to cool before taking a sip. His eyes rolled back in intense pleasure. The coffee was perfect. It was strong, but not too strong; bitter and sweet at the same time. It was exactly what Alex had always looked for in a cup of coffee. He was in love.

Stuck

I failed again. Another F to add to my stack of failed papers from Business 201. My teacher had warned me this was my last chance. She told me that if I managed to receive at least a C on this paper I still had a chance to raise my grade to a passing level. And I failed.

My freshman year, I'd barely scraped by. I had tried, too, dutifully taking notes and studying for tests. This year was even worse. It doesn't seem to matter how hard I try. The only class that I'm still passing, barely, is Aeronautics: the Science of Flight, a simple General Education class.

I gather my books and shove the paper in the trash. As I walk across campus, I think about what I will tell my parents. They already think of me as a failure. I am the youngest of their four kids and the only one who has ever had any trouble in school. My sister and brothers were all straight A's. I barely made it into college. That's me: the failure. At least I'm living up to their expectations.

I've always been the odd one out, the black sheep. And not just with my family. Everywhere I go, I never seem to fit in.

I briefly consider skipping my next class and going home to brood. I picture myself curled up in bed with a mug of hot chocolate. But the next class is Aeronautics, and I don't want to jeopardize my one passing grade. Plus, our class has been constructing small planes for the past two weeks and I really want to finish mine.

In Aeronautics class, I immediately get to work, concentrating hard on trying to make the plane fly. Near the end of the class, it finally lifts off, soaring above the table and around the room. I watch it glide above the rest of the class. My classmates are all still working on their planes. As it rises higher, I feel a mixture of both happiness at seeing the plane take off and jealousy that I am still stuck on the floor.

"High five!" yells my lab partner, slapping my hand. His name is Theo. He is a tall senior with dreadlocks and warm eyes. He is not the best at Aeronautics, but he tries hard.

"I'm having a party tonight," he says to me as we pack up our things. "You should come. It's gonna be fun!"

I briefly wonder why someone would have a party on a Tuesday night, but I'm also aware that he's waiting for an answer.

"Sounds good. I'll try to make it." I don't have any real intention of going.

"Awesome! I will see you then," he says, taking my lack of conviction for a yes. He writes down the address and hands me the piece of paper.

I go home and lie in bed, wondering what to do next with my life. Should I drop out before I fail out? I've disliked college since the first day: the classes, the other students, the teachers. But if I drop out, what will I do? What kind of job could I get? When I was little, I wanted to be an astronaut, but then I discovered how many years of school and science classes it would require. And with my grades, it was clear that career path was not going to be a possibility.

I lie there for the rest of the afternoon feeling sorry for myself. Around the time the sun goes down, I hear a knock on my bedroom door. It's my roommate.

"Hey, Ashley, I'm having some friends over tonight. Is that cool with you?"

"I'm not really feeling up to a party tonight. Plus, it's Tuesday," I say, knowing she's going to have her friends over no matter what I say.

"Oh come on, it'll be fun. You don't even have to be here, if you don't want to."

"I..."

"Thanks!" she interrupts me and runs off.

I hate my roommate's friends. They're all loud, obnoxious freshmen who spend their time getting trashed and listening to bad hip-hop music. Great, I think, this is just what I need.

I consider going to Theo's party and I immediately start to feel nervous about it. I won't know anyone except Theo.

I decide not to go. But then I hear a knock on the apartment door and shortly after the loud voice of one of my roommate's friends yells "Party!" and goes on about the cheap vodka that she convinced some older boy to buy for her.

I'll go to Theo's, I decide. I can't stay here, and I really don't have anywhere else to go. Plus, Theo was under the impression that I was going to go, so it would be rude not to stop by.

Reluctantly, I start to get dressed. I'm surprised to find that I have no going-out clothes. I try to remember the last time that I went to a party. Maybe a year ago, I think. I settle on clean-enough jeans and a purple hoodie—comfort over fashion, as usual.

I live right off of campus, as does Theo. In fact, Google Maps tells me that his house is only a 10-minute walk from my apartment. I write directions on a sticky note and walk out the door, avoiding any contact with my roommate or her friends.

It only takes me about five minutes to get lost. I'm supposed to turn on Shaver Street, but I can't find it. I take a left at a street that I'm guessing might be near Theo's house, but it's a dead end, and the next one is, too. I think I might be walking in circles. I soon realize that I no longer know how to find my way home. After wandering around for a few minutes, I find myself on a street lined with older, slightly rundown houses. There are students overflowing on the porches, drinking cheap beers. It seems promising to me; I continue walking down it. Soon enough, I hit another dead end. A concrete wall stares directly at me, mocking me. It's not too tall, though. I walk up to it and stand on my tiptoes to see over. The street on the other side looks familiar. That's it, I decide; that's where I need to be.

There's an empty dog house to my right. I pull myself on top of it and hop over the wall. Looking around, I quickly realize that I was wrong. This place isn't familiar at all. The houses are much nicer on this side of the wall. They are all modern, built from the same cookie-cutter design. This is definitely not Theo's street. I turn around, thinking to climb back over the wall, but there is nothing to use as a step stool here. I'll have to walk back around. I start walking down the road, hoping it might take me where I want to be.

I try to lift my feet from the road, but they're stuck. The white rubber bottoms of my Converse sneakers are melting into the charcoal-colored asphalt. Or maybe it's the other way around—maybe it's the asphalt that is oozing up to engulf the rubber soles. Straining, I lift a foot, but the road sucks it back down. Groaning, I pull harder and suddenly stumble forward as the connection breaks. I nearly fall and my hand grazes the road. The congealing surface grabs the skin of my palms and attempts to suck me down. I yank my hand back, rolling off the road and onto the dirt. The stream of asphalt that had been clinging to me snaps back violently to rejoin the road. My heart is racing. I wait there, frozen, but the asphalt is motionless. I examine my hand: it is normal again, and so are the bottoms of my sneakers.

I stand up. The dirt is just dirt. It doesn't try to capture my feet. It allows me to continue my walk and doesn't seem to be offended by my feet pressing down to emboss waffle-patterned footprints on its surface. I stand for a second, marveling at how perfectly the soles of my shoes impress their shape in the soft dirt. I walk beside the road, following its curves and bends, but careful not to set foot on it.

I'm only briefly aware that I have forgotten where I'm heading, as well as where I came from. I'm only interested in where this road is leading me, and that has yet to be determined.

A gutter fixes its gaze on me from the side of the road. Its pitch-black interior reflects the light from the night sky like faint gold glitter. The metal bars waver slightly. I bend down to look inside and see only a dark void. I want to reach my hand inside, but I'm afraid that I might not be able to recover it. I turn away and suddenly I'm blinded by two bright lights speeding toward me. The wind whips by, pulling me in all directions as the black car zooms past. I shrink away from this arrogant, mechanical object, which seems to me a defect in the world—something that should not be here at all.

I resume my walk. It feels as though I have been walking for hours, but when I turn my head back, I can still see the place where my footsteps began in the dirt, right next to where the asphalt melts.

A house slightly different from the others on the street grabs my attention. I stop. It's not the appearance of the house that marks it as different because all the houses on this street look exactly the same: two-story, white-brick squares covered with brown-shingled roofs. I look into the house's two paneled eyes that are shaded by white coverings. I sense there is something inside the house, something that I cannot see, but that makes this place different from all the ones that look just like it.

"Where am I going?" I ask the house.

I half expect the door to open in reply, but the house maintains its dark silence. I want desperately to walk up the steps and open the front door to find my answer, but the steps are quicksand now. The brown-and-tan grains swirl in counterclockwise patterns on each stair. Climbing them will not be an option. I back away from the house, stopping right before my shoe touches the asphalt.

I struggle to remember which direction I've come from. Am I lost? I try to remember where I was going and how I got here, but that part of my mind has gone blank. There is a rapid beating in my chest and adrenaline pulses through me. I'm lost! Which way should I go?

To my right I see my own footsteps in the dirt. They are directed straight toward me. I step back onto that path and continue in the same direction I was heading. I lose count of my steps, but I stop when I reach an intersection. The road separates into two opposite paths. To my left, the road is lined with houses, all with unblinking eyes and closed mouths. They watch me with silent and cold dispassion.

The road to my right is lined with trees. They reach out their branches to me, shaking their leaves and beckoning me onward.

As I walk to the right, the trees reach out their branches, closer and closer, toward me. One strokes me lightly on the shoulder. I jump, almost stumbling back onto the road. My eyes move to the offending tree and I glimpse a slight depression in the ground beside it that appears to be a narrow path. It's barely discernible, but it leads into a wooded area. I can see the outline of the trees in the distance lit up by the stars and moon above.

Filled with curiosity, I turn down the slender trail. The tree branches wave and beckon me into their grove, shaking their leaves impatiently. They're right, I think; this is my path. The wind is lighter here. The trees have formed a barrier against it. I feel lighter here, too.

A few yards down the trail, I'm careful not to step in the dark blue puddle in the middle of the path. One can only guess how deep it might be. Curious, I kneel down and examine my reflection. A girl gazes back. Her hair is the same long length as mine, but not quite the right shade of black. Her eyes are just as blue as mine, but their shape is distorted from the almond outline of my own. I open my mouth and say "Hello." She opens her mouth too, but no words reach the air. The pale reflection simply stares back at me. I feel a shiver of fear. There is something almost menacing about her. I look at the red glasses on her nose, the purple sweatshirt covering her torso and the dark mascara lining her eyelashes. My body shakes uncontrollably and I have to look away because my reflection isn't me. It's someone I've been turned into by society, by what others expect. I spring to my feet and step around the puddle. I continue moving deeper into the grove.

The stars and moon kindly give me plenty of light so I can make out my surroundings. I stop in my tracks to ponder the illuminating sky.

"Well, hello there," says a voice a few feet above me.

"Hello to you, too," I reply to the tree. It is by far the widest and tallest tree that I have yet come across in this grove. The grooved bark of the old tree shifts around to form a small, polite smile. Above the smile, two holes sink deep into its core, forming eyes that gaze at me with a deep kindness. There is something feminine about this tree, I think to myself.

"May I ask," I begin, striving to remain polite to such a stately tree, "what a talking tree is doing in the middle of this grove, in the middle of a large city?"

"Harrumm!" says the tree, "I suppose I could ask you, my dear, what a young girl is doing in such a small grove in the middle of a large city."

"In all honesty, I'm not quite sure."

"Oh," replies the tree. Its eyes grow slightly smaller scrutinizing me. "Well, you see, I have a very good reason for being in such a small grove in such a large city: I am stuck."

"Stuck?"

"My roots reach deep down into the soil. They are embedded there, and though I have tried, I cannot seem to move them." The tree shakes its branches in agitation. I duck down to avoid being swiped by one.

"Your roots, however," the tree continues, "are not stuck. You are free to move about. So what is your reason for coming here?"

I gaze down at the blue Converse sneakers that enclose my

two small feet. The once-white laces are tinted green with grass stain. I lift one foot up and shake it slightly. It is not stuck. No roots are holding me here. The tree has a very good point.

"I guess I'm looking for something."

"What is this *something* that you are looking for?" asks the tree.

"I'm not quite sure. I believe it's something that I've been looking for, for a long time."

"Oh well, I suppose if you are looking for something you should not be dallying. Do continue your search, but please come back and visit me again before you leave."

Obediently, I turn to walk away, but I turn around for one last question: "Are you lonely, Miss Tree?"

"Lonely?" she rustles gently. "Why would I be lonely? I have the birds, the squirrels, the insects and all the other trees, although I may be the only one who can talk." The tree sighs. "Okay, yes, I do get lonely sometimes."

"I get lonely, too," I admit.

"Why would you get lonely? Are you not surrounded by others like yourself—humans who can talk, just like you?"

The tree has a point. I think about it briefly.

"There are no others like myself. If there are, I haven't found them."

"Perhaps that may have something to do with the thing you are searching for?" the tree suggests.

"Yes," I say.

"Anyways, on with you!" She dismisses me with a wave of her twigs. "You must go and find what you are looking for."

"Thank you! I'll come back," I promise, striding away.

Past the old tree, the ground begins to slope downward. I proceed carefully, but my feet are sure on this path and I feel quite safe in this grove, even though I can no longer see the road. I walk down the slope and listen to the calls from the nocturnal birds and the calming voices of the insects around me. Their songs and simple melodies fill me with warmth. I realize I've shaken off the deep chill that encompassed me when I was walking along the road and hearing tires rolling over the asphalt. I shudder slightly remembering the asphalt, and the way it tried so desperately to trap me.

In this grove I feel safe. The grass I'm walking on is friendly. It won't try to suck me into it. I will not get stuck in this grove. I feel my heart beat strong and confident.

How long have I been wandering through these trees? Has it been hours? Days? Weeks? Years? I can no longer tell.

I come upon a narrow creek. The small trickle of water reflects the dusty-black night sky, stirred by the pale yellow reflection from the celestial bodies above. I gaze into the water, evading the stare of the reflection that looks up at me. It frightens me to see my own reflection. The features are too common and the eyes are too solemn. She looks like every other person. But it's a lie, because I'm not like them. I focus on the ridges of the small ripples skating across the top of the creek.

"Be careful not to fall in," a voice behind me says. Startled, I almost do.

"Oh, sorry," the voice says. "I should have introduced myself before I interrupted your thoughts. They must be pretty deep, the way you have been staring into that creek."

I turn to face a tree. Its face, fashioned of warped bark shaped into a light smile, is quite similar to the tree I've already spoken with.

"You're not the tree I talked to before?" I ask it, a little confused.

"I do not think you and I have ever met." Its eyes widen slightly, looking me over carefully. "Yes," the tree continues, "if we had met before, I would recognize you. You see, I can recognize anyone whom I have met before. It is quite a talent."

I move closer to the tree to get a better look. It's definitely not the same talking tree. This one's trunk doesn't stretch as wide as the other tree, which had been quite plump. Also, the bark of this tree has a lighter tinge. This tree must be younger than the other one. It's not even as tall as the other, silent, trees that surround us. It probably grew from the seed of one of the older trees nearby.

"I'm sorry, I must have been mistaken," I say politely to the new tree. "You see, I've recently met another talking tree who said that she was the only tree around who could talk to me."

"Well, that is pretty strange. I thought *I* was the only talking tree around. Where is this other tree?"

I point. "It's right up that hill."

"Oh, how interesting. I would very much like to meet this tree. Unfortunately, I cannot move from this spot." The tree shakes its branches with annoyance. It twists its trunk from side to side, but remains stuck to its spot. "Well, at least now I know there is another tree like me around. I will not feel so lonely."

I feel sympathetic as I watch the tree try to unearth its roots. I know how it feels to be surrounded by others who can't understand me, to have no one else like me around, and to want to go somewhere where my roots won't allow me to go.

"I'll tell the other tree that you're here as well," I promise, impulsively laying my hand on the tree's rough bark. "Then she'll also know that she's not alone."

"Thank you."

"Sir," I say, because this tree's voice is much deeper than the first tree's, "do you often talk to people who come through your grove?"

"I do," the tree tells me, "but no one has ever responded before."

"But you didn't seem surprised that I could hear you," I say.

"Yes," he agrees. "Just because it had not happened before did not make me doubt that it could happen someday."

"I'm impressed," I tell the talking tree. "I've never been that good at holding on to hope. I've always given up."

"The best part of hope is that you can always reach for it, even if you have not before. It is always there."

I think about that for a few minutes as we both enjoy the silence. The tree finally breaks it.

"Erm, if I may ask, what hope did you give up on in the past?"

I think about the tree's question as I gaze at the moon. The golden light is brighter than any of the city's street lights. I wish that I could get closer, see it up close. I briefly remember feeling this way when I was younger, yearning to be so close to the moon that I could touch it. I attempt to answer the tree, but find myself wordless.

"I suggest you walk deeper into the forest," the tree says gently. "There is where you will find the birds. They always seem to know where they are going."

"I will. Goodbye," I say to the tree. "Thank you."

"Good luck."

I cross the stream and the sloping ground levels out. The grove thickens and I have to duck under the branches to avoid their graze against my face and arms. When I accidentally snap a low branch, I cringe, remembering the talking trees. However, this tree remains silent.

Suddenly, I come to a small clearing in the forest. I lie down in the center. Through the branches I look up at the stars above me. The pinpoints of light call to me and I feel their familiar pull. But I'm still too heavy, weighed down by useless gravity.

An owl swoops down and lands next to my head.

"I didn't expect to find anyone here," the owl says to me, slightly affronted.

"I'm sorry. Is this meadow yours? I didn't mean to intrude."

"Oh no, dear, not mine! This is the earth. The ground can't possibly belong to anyone."

The grass happily tickles the center of my palms at the owl's words.

"Do you like it?" I ask the owl, returning my eyes to the night sky.

"Like what?"

"Being able to fly up there, up in the sky."

"Ah, yes," the owl replies with a feathery sigh. "It is absolute perfection to soar about through the air feeling the wind beneath my wings."

"You can go anywhere?" I ask the owl.

"I can. Like the wind, there are no boundaries I cannot cross."

"That sounds so perfect," I sigh heavily. "I've never met anyone who wasn't restricted by boundaries."

"I have watched you people," the owl admits. "You are constantly putting up fences and building walls. Yet, you are the ones who must walk around them! We birds have no need of those things. The world is wide open to me. I need no open gates or doorways to my freedom."

"I once thought that the world was wide open to me, too,"
I say. "When I was younger, I wanted more than anything
to fly up to the stars, to be able to see the whole universe.
But now I spend my life squeezing through gates and fences,
trapped in classrooms and behind closed windows. I spend
my days staring at walls, but I want the stars! Have you ever
flown that high? High enough to visit the stars?"

"Oh no!" the owl hoots with amusement. "I don't believe
I could possibly fly that far." I feel deflated, but then the
owl adds, "I did have a cousin who flew so high that he just
disappeared. Who knows where he is now?"

My spirits lift. "He must have visited the stars and found
the most unimaginable things! I believe they have lights and
music up there that we can't possibly conceive of down here."

"I suspect so," the owl agrees. "It would explain why he
has not come back down."

"Have you ever thought about flying up there and trying
to find him?"

"No, I am content down here," the owl says, "but what
about you?"

"Me?"

"Are you content down here?"

I know the answer to that right away. "No. I don't like it
down here." I realize I'm more comfortable in this grove than
I've ever felt in the city or at school, but even now I feel rest-
less and incomplete.

"You are human," says the owl. "The cities were made for
you. Why do you not feel content there?"

"It's cold and dead in the city. It pulls me in and traps me
and I'm afraid that I'll be stuck forever."

Another owl hoots off in the distance.

"That is my sister," the owl says. "I feel my place is here, just as I'm sure my cousin felt his was someplace far away, someplace that he could only find by flying away into the sky."

A small butterfly floats by my face. Its wings are a swirl of the deepest blues and brightest greens waving back and forward through the air, moving to and fro. It is so beautiful, and so much freer than I will ever be.

"If you are curious about my cousin, talk to the oldest tree in the grove," suggests the owl. "My cousin often visited her."

"Thank you," I say.

"You're welcome. Now I must be going." Another hoot from a different owl breaks the air. "The sun will rise soon and my family is calling."

The owl flies away, leaving me once again alone in the clearing. I rise from my spot. The dark night has started to grow a fraction lighter, shedding a pre-dawn glow over the grove. I look down where my body has left a small indent in the grass to show that I had been there. The right direction seems clear to me now and I walk quickly.

By the time I reach the oldest tree in the forest, the call of the morning birds is starting.

"Hello," I say to the tree.

"Well, you have returned," she greets me.

"I met another tree like you. He talked to me, too."

"He did?" The tree's bark mouth bends into a smile. "Well, thank you for telling me. It is nice to know that I'm not the only one. Did you find what you were looking for?"

"What I need isn't here. But I think it will be okay."

"Will it?" she asks me. There is no surprise in her voice.

"Yes, because I know *you* can help me find it! The owl told me about his cousin who flew to the stars."

The tree is silent. I need her to understand. "Please! In the city, I'm surrounded by humans, and yes we can talk, but not one of them understands me; not one of them is like me! I only ever feel lonely. In the city, I can't reach the stars. I can't ever see what's above the sky because I'm not the sort of human who will ever be allowed to fly a plane or take a rocket to the moon." Tears run down my cheeks. "I'm only suited to be a dreamer. And I can't get to the stars by dreaming alone."

"You are stuck," the tree murmurs, rustling its leaves sympathetically.

"I am! If I go back to the city, I have a duty to live up to the expectations of my family. They will expect me to be like all the other humans, and I'm not." I'm not. That has always been the problem. I'm stuck being me, and I need to find a way to be myself and be free. "Please help me," I say, throwing my arms around the tree.

"Once you go there is no turning back," she warns.

I take a deep breath and then another. I feel steady. In the distance I can see faint lights on the road that leads back to the city. A sense of relief fills me because I know I will not be returning there.

"Come," says the tree. "Press your back against my bark. This will not hurt a bit."

I do as she says and she draws me in. My back sinks into her pith.

The tree's voice is as close as my own. "Good luck, little one," she whispers as her bark looses me and her branches gently lift me under each arm. They raise me up into the air and throw me to the sky. The sun breaks over the horizon with dazzling yellow light as I tumble higher and higher through the air.

I reach my arms up and they sprout feathers and fan out beside me, sleek and sure. I know just what to do. I look straight ahead. I beat my wings and aim for the stars.

Ambition

It's hard not to reflect on your life when you're floating a hundred feet above the ground. Sandwiched in between Snoopy and the Pillsbury Doughboy, I look down at the thousands of people, all specks on the streets far below, and try to remember how the hell I got here.

"Ambition," my grandfather used to say, "is a powerful tool. A lot of great men have wasted their lives, dwindling to nothing because of lack of ambition."

My grandfather would usually take a pause here, suck on his cigar and slowly breathe out the smoke. I always liked how the white vapor moved about in the air, curling and rising up to the ceiling.

"Your father," my grandfather would continue, "now, he is a prime example of a man who wasted his life because of his lack of ambition."

I'd fidget a little. I thought my father was a good man. He never hit me, never lost his temper, always went to work on time (although never early), and always ate dinner at the table with his family and never in front of the TV.

"He could have been so much more," my grandfather would say, fixing me with a stare, "a real successful man, rather than a small-time office worker, if only he had more ambition! And then he went and married your mother, no offense to her of course, but he could have done so much better. Your father was quite the looker in his time, just like you'll be." And then my grandfather would wink one of his crinkly brown eyes at me.

My father seemed perfectly content with his life of no ambition. He made a decent living at his job, but never aspired to make more. In fact, when he was offered a promotion at his company for quite a bit more money, he turned it down because it would have required him to spend his Saturdays at the office, and my father was a family man. He never put in more than the necessary 40 hours, and he worked fewer hours when he could.

As for my mom, well it was common knowledge that my grandfather was not particularly fond of her. She wasn't bad looking by any means, but she wasn't drop-dead gorgeous. She was always kind and loving. She had been a great mom to me and a great wife to my father, but in my grandfather's opinion that was not enough. My grandfather wholeheartedly believed that my dad should not have settled for anything less than America's Next Top Model. He ignored the reality that my father was only 5 feet 10 inches, and those girls would have towered over him—especially in heels.

My mom, on the other hand, was 5 feet 3 inches and had always been in quite good shape. My parents truly loved each other. They enjoyed holding hands and they rarely fought or nagged each other. My mother and my father made a decently attractive and more-than-happy couple.

But my grandfather, he never saw a happy couple. All he saw was a son with no ambition and the woman his son settled for. And it did not take long for me, being of an impressionable age and spending every summer with the man, to begin to see my parents that way as well.

Thank whatever god might be out there, we have started to move again! For a while there I worried that I would never get my head out of Snoopy's ass. It would actually be nice up here if it wasn't so goddamn cold. When you're watching it on TV, you can see all the people on the ground in their warm coats and scarves, and you figure that they're cold. But what the pretty reporter never tells you is how much colder it is up here, where the balloons are.

Also, there's not much to do up here. It's pretty boring, actually. You can't hear the music, you can't see the other balloons because you're stuck in line, and the people are too small to make out. The only thing to do, really, is to stare at Snoopy's ass. I've had enough of his big, white, dog butt for the day.

The only thing left to do is to reflect on ambition. That's how I got up here, after all.

What my father lacked in ambition I made up for tenfold, thanks to my grandfather.

Unfortunately, I was never really all that bright to begin with. I tried for the top grades in my class, but despite my hard work I was lucky if I even ranked in the top half. Even with the extra tutoring I took after school and hours I spent in the library and help from my mom at home (she was always quite good at math), I always ended up with a C average at the end of the semester. Not that my parents cared—they were just happy that I was trying so hard. They never complained that I was not bringing home A's and B's.

In middle school, I started playing basketball. I wanted with all my heart to be the team captain and would spend all my free time practicing in the school gym. But no matter how hard I tried to be a great ballplayer, most of my game time was spent on the bench.

I wasn't that handsome either, despite what my grandfather told me. I was closer to my mother's height than my father's, my forehead was a little big, and my nose too small. But I still became the pickiest son of a bitch when it came to women. I wanted to ask Michelle to prom in high school. She was the most beautiful girl in the class, captain of the cheerleaders, best dressed and smart, too. I planned an elaborate scheme in which I gave her a kitten with the word "Prom?" shaved in its fur. I put it in her locker (don't worry, there were air holes). But it turned out that Michelle was allergic to cats, and having put the newly shaved feline on top of all her school books, I managed to get cat hair on everything in her locker. She spent the next week sneezing constantly, and I ended up not even attending prom.

In retrospect, I should have gone to prom with Bobbi, who had apparently wanted me to ask her. She'd told her friend Sarah, who had left me a note in my gym bag about it. But Bobbi wasn't very pretty, and her grades were worse than mine. I thought she was nice, but I had resolved never to settle. I had high ambitions for myself.

I should have learned from my mistakes. If I had, I might not be where I am right now, a 38-year-old dateless semi-virgin. But instead of getting wiser, I kept making the same mistakes over and over, trying to date the girls who looked down on me and ignoring the girls who looked up to me.

Not only is it cold up here, it's windy, too. And man, was that quite the gust! It hit Pillsbury so hard that he rammed his white chef's hat straight into the back of my knee. These balloons may only be filled with helium, but they still weigh a few hundred pounds. I'm going to be sore for a month.

❧

I tried to go to college after high school. My parents advised me to apply to the local community college, but that would have been settling. I only applied to Ivy League schools. Of course, I was rejected from them all. So I decided to gain some valuable work experience before I reapplied. I was confident that it would not take long for me to work my way up in any business and becomes its CEO, and then those Ivy snobs would beg me to attend their exclusive schools. I landed a minimum wage job slinging burgers at a fast food restaurant. When I lost that job, I bagged groceries, and after I was fired I mopped floors after closing time at a neighborhood bar. When I lost that job, I landed a shift as a gas station attendant. I told myself it was only temporary. That was 19 years ago.

My plan was always to work my way up to manager of the gas station, and then to own my own station and then a hundred stations. I would have my own corporate headquarters with a corner office and personal assistant. In reality, my manager was much younger than I was and had no intention of leaving any time soon because his uncle owned the gas station. But I still clung to my belief that ambition was all I needed to succeed.

Then, exactly one year ago to the day, I was alone—as usual—in my tiny, one-bedroom apartment. I had the day off and was watching the Macy's Thanksgiving Day Parade, just as I did every Thanksgiving. My parents had passed away a few years back—within the same month, actually—and my grandfather had been gone for nearly 20 years (although his influence on me is quite permanent). I was all alone in the world, sitting on my salmon-pink couch with the big hole down the middle, when she came on the screen. It was in between one very peppy high school marching band and a float for sick children. Her hair was perfect—long, blonde and wavy; her eyes sparkled blue and her lips were just the right shade of red. When she let out a breathy giggle and began to talk in her perfect, made-for-TV voice, I knew I was in love. The graphic in the corner of the TV identified her as Tiffany Mayfair.

I thought I had been in love a few times before, but this was the real thing—the big one, the life changer. I knew it once I saw her perfectly manicured fingernails. I had to be with this woman. Nothing would get in the way of my ambition this time.

Day and night, Tiffany occupied my mind constantly. In my daydreams, we would go sailing on the French Riviera, picnic in Central Park, and make love in elegant villas in Italy. In my mind, she was mine. But after a month of fantasizing, I grew frustrated. Thinking about her wasn't enough; I had to be with her in the real world. That's when I came up with a plan to sweep the lovely newscaster off her feet. I spent the greater half of my latest paycheck to rent a black tuxedo and I bought two dozen satin roses—the kind that would never die (just like my love for Tiffany).

The next morning, I showed up at the studio, roses in hand, dressed in my crisp tuxedo with a fresh hair cut and expensive aftershave lotion. But the security guard at the door wouldn't let me inside. I waited all day long on the curb, but I didn't see her come out. For the next month, I showed up at the TV studio every single day. I trimmed my hair once a week and spent a fortune taking the tuxedo to the nearby dry cleaners every other day, to keep it crisp. But despite my determination, I never saw her—not in person, at least. I could still watch her to my heart's content on TV, which I did every night until I fell asleep. But that wasn't what I wanted.

On Day 37 of my stakeout, something hit me. It was that jerk guarding the door, to be exact. In my extreme frustration, I tried to rush past him and he knocked me down with one arm. I lay on the gravel trying to catch my breath when the jerk came over and actually held out his hand to help me up.

"I guess I shouldn't have hit you quite that hard. You are a little guy after all," he said apologetically, brushing dirt off my silk-lined jacket. "But you can't just rush into a television studio like that."

"But I have to tell Tiffany that I love her!"

"Do you really think you can win Tiffany's heart with a bouquet of fake flowers and a dirty tuxedo?"

"It wasn't dirty before I got knocked down," I grumbled.

"You're going to need something bigger than that," the jerk said to me, nodding to the flowers that were still clutched tightly in my hand and looked wilted despite the fact that they weren't even real.

"How much bigger?" I asked him. I thought about bringing a tree or a rose bush.

"Bigger than you could ever get."

Well, that's when it came to me. The parade balloons! The first time I'd seen her, Tiffany had gushed enthusiastically about the giant balloons bobbing down Fifth Avenue. I could still remember her excited smile as she described each balloon as it swept past.

I could already see it. There she would be, enthusing over the fat Santa, when all of a sudden she'd be swept away by a declaration of love from one of the parade's own balloons. She wouldn't be able to resist me. I was sure of it! In that moment, my ambition grew bigger than it had ever grown before.

Being struck with inspiration was one thing, but executing the plan successfully was another. I'd had a lot of experience with this phenomenon in the past. And while I now knew how I could win Tiffany's heart, I was not quite sure how to go about it.

Luckily, I still had nine months and two weeks until Thanksgiving. That gave me just enough time for planning.

I'd lost my job at the gas station after the first week of staking out the TV studio, but it didn't bother me. I'd inherited enough money from my parents to live on for at least a year. I hadn't spent any of it yet because I had been saving it for a trip around the world. I'd planned to visit every single country in the world and woo one girl in each place. Oh, the dreams of a semi-virgin.

I figured now was the time to dig into my savings. After all, once I was with Tiffany, my life would be golden. I would get a better job, make tons of cash, have lots of friends and all my life's ambitions would finally be fulfilled. So I focused myself full-time on achieving my new goal.

It was clear that elasticity was what I would need first and foremost if I truly wanted to turn myself into a giant message balloon of love for my Tiffany. But how does a man go about making himself elastic? In my case, the man first goes to the library. I spent two solid weeks skimming through book after book that referenced elasticity. I was well-acquainted with the library, having spent so much time in it in my younger days. Although it hadn't turned me into an

Honor Roll student, it did give me some skills at finding the books I needed.

During my two weeks of reading, I thumbed through science books, fiction books, non-fiction books and history books. By the end, I'd sketched out a plan the likes of which would make any elementary school science fair winner turn green with envy.

My first step was to buy chewing gum. I went to the grocery store and filled two carts with assorted varieties of gum. Not wanting to tire myself out on one flavor, I tossed in mint, raspberry, fruit stripe (the one with the zebra on the pack), cinnamon, lemon-lime and every other flavor that looked interesting. Sugarless, sugar-free, extra sugar—all of it went into my shopping cart, along with two bottles of cheap vodka. At the checkout counter I began to feel awkward for the first time since starting my new project.

"I know how this may look," I said to the woman with the long face and brown-haired ponytail.

"Don't worry," she said as she scanned a box of Bazooka (I was looking forward to those the most, for the comics). "I've seen much stranger purchases than two carts of gum and cheap vodka."

After the supermarket, I went down to the gym near my house to sign up for three different yoga classes. Elasticity requires stretchability, an aptitude I have always lacked.

My final stop was the fabric store—a place I had never been before—where I purchased two different-sized needles and a very large amount of blue thread. Blue has always been my favorite color.

Oh no, I think I'm beginning to feel nauseous! It's this

incessant shaking motion. Those handlers down there, they have no idea what they're doing. They're just waving me back and forth, no consideration at all. All the pain I went through, and this is what I get.

The first step was to chew the gum. All 15,360 pieces of gum would have to be chewed thoroughly before they would be workable. Eventually, my jaw got so sore that I began to wonder if I would have to spend the rest of my life on a liquid diet. (Whether or not I will be able to ingest solid foods again—well, only time will tell.)

They say when you swallow gum it stays in your body for up to five years. I figured by the time I was 43, I would be back to my normal size and shape. Five years, I could deal with that. Five years was not that much time. So I chewed the gum, but I didn't swallow it yet. Instead, I kept it in the oven, already chewed, so it would stay malleable. The plan was to swallow it all at once. That's where the vodka came in.

Just swallowing gum wouldn't be adequate. To make room for the gum, I'd have to let myself out. After all, I didn't want to explode—I wanted to balloon. This was the key to my plan. I swallowed enough vodka until I couldn't feel the pain if I pricked the tip of my finger. Then I picked up the sharpest kitchen knife I had and, well, I won't go into detail, but I now have 12 different lines of stitches in various parts of my body, all places where skin has been sewn together with blue thread. The thread was advertised as being unbreakable no matter how much pressure it's under. I am counting on that being true.

By the time all the gum was chewed and I was all sewn up, the pain was mostly a memory. It was only three days until the Macy's Thanksgiving Day Parade. I had taken my final yoga class that morning. I'd gotten quite good at not only the Tree pose, but also the Dancer and Sun Salutation. It was time to start swallowing the gum. I ate it in chunks about the size of a disco ball for breakfast, lunch, dinner and snacks. The evening before Thanksgiving—just yesterday, in fact—I gulped down the last chunk.

My body, which had always been a very pale and pasty white color, turned bright pink in some places, and mint green in others. My toes all turned rainbow thanks to the zebra fruit stripe gum.

I've lived in Hoboken, New Jersey my whole life, just across the Hudson River from New York City, but I'd never been to the Macy's Thanksgiving Day Parade. This morning, I woke up at the crack of dawn and donned a pair of black spandex pants and t-shirt—the most stretchable that I could find. Technically, these are women's clothing, but no one needs to know that.

There was still one more piece to my plan that I had to execute. I had to be able to float.

I took the early-morning train from Trenton, New Jersey straight to Penn Station. I'd forgotten it was on the holiday schedule, and I started to worry that I was going to be too late. I hurried through Penn Station and jumped on the subway heading uptown. From studying the parade map on the Macy's website, I knew exactly where to get off to reach the parade prep area. I needed to get into the tent where they kept the helium.

This was the part of the plan I had to improvise. I could not afford to be noticed by the parade officials because if I got kicked out of the parade prep grounds I would never pull off my scheme. Luckily for me, all the parade workers had "high" aspirations of their own because they were too busy passing around some fat joints to notice me sliding under the canvas of the helium tent. Then it was a simple matter of crawling to the nearest helium tank and starting to suck.

The gum was clearly doing its job. I could feel my skin stretching, but it didn't hurt. My body expanded more and more with each gulp of the gas. Closing my eyes, I enjoyed the light-headed feeling. By the time I opened my eyes, the tap was empty and I was 70 feet long. I pulled up my shirt and saw I was almost translucent in the middle. I was also floating in the air, and I bumped my head a few times against the top of the tent.

"Oh no!" I heard one of the parade workers yell. "That one is about to get away!" They all laughed as they looked up at me. One of them pulled out a very tall ladder and climbed to the top. He attached several ropes to my green fingers and rainbow toes (which might have tickled had I any sensation left in my extremities). He tied the ends of the ropes to stakes at the bottom of the tent, and I floated there just like the other balloons that were already in the tent.

"In a hurry to get out?" one of the workers said to me. "Don't worry, you'll be able to fly with your fellows soon enough."

Even as a balloon, I was still ambitious because ambition doesn't die just because you balloon out to 70 feet. If anything, it grows with you.

As I waited to be released from my stakes, I started planning my confession of love to Tiffany. I wanted to tell her, face to face, how I felt about her, but I realized I was too high off the ground for her to hear me. I would have to do it when the telephoto lenses of the TV cameras focused on me. I hadn't prepared a speech, but I figured the words would come to me. I wasn't too worried. After all, I was going to be the biggest man she'd ever seen, so there was no way she could possibly resist me now. And once the helium died down, I would re-stretch to roughly my normal size, and she and I could be together, finally.

It was not long until I and my fellow balloons were released from the ropes that bound us to the ground. A swarm of muscle-bound young men grabbed the ends of the ropes that were attached to my fingers. As they pulled me out, they carelessly held me too high and bumped my forehead on the top of the tarp.

I opened my mouth to yell at them to watch where they were going, but no words came out. Instead, a light pink bubble, the color of Bazooka chewing gum, escaped from my lips. I tried again and again to let out a noise, but the only things that came out were more little pink bubbles. Frantic, I tried to wave my arms and legs, but I only felt more distraught when I found that I couldn't move any of my limbs, not even a little. As they launched me into the parade, I suddenly remembered that I'm deathly afraid of heights.

So this is where ambition got me: multicolored, mute, paralyzed and stretched beyond my limits—all in the name of love.

The Day the World Collapsed.

The Day the World Collapsed

The day the world collapsed, Kurt woke up with a hangover. He untangled himself from his red satin sheets and placed his slightly large feet on the plush carpet covering his Manhattan condo. Then he dragged himself to the next room to make a pot of coffee, spilling the coffee beans onto the floor. By the time he cleaned it up he was already late for work, although he was not particularly worried about it. Kurt gave up on breakfast, not feeling hungry anyway, and hopped into the shower. He scrubbed away the sour smells of alcohol and cigar smoke that seemed still to be oozing from the pores of his skin. He lathered his hair twice to shed the odor as he tried desperately to remember the night before.

⚜

To anybody watching, Kurt Riley Colveman looked like just one more drunk businessman who spent night after night sitting alone in a bar with a constant glass of vodka in his hand. To anybody watching, Kurt Riley Colveman was just another depressed soul stuck in a life he never wanted; hopeless and destined to be miserable for the rest of his life. But nobody was watching Kurt Riley Colveman. That was the problem as he sat alone in a bar wasting his large paycheck on mediocre vodka.

Kurt was not a stupid man. He already knew how he must look to others, and how alone he was and that it was his own damn fault. He knew a lot of other things as well. He knew more about Excel spreadsheets than anybody else in his office. He also knew the stats of all of the players on the New York Yankees since 1988, and how to draw a perfectly round circle. He knew basic and advanced math (but still could not divide without a calculator). He knew how to mix paints to form the perfect shade of red—somewhere between the color of blood and a dark merlot.

With all of this knowledge, Kurt walked into Rum Bar one lonely Tuesday night. He had just come from work and was still wearing his tailored, dark-chocolate-colored suit; white-linen, long-sleeved shirt; and shiny, black-silk tie, which matched his shoes. His hair was the exact color of his suit and he wore it parted straight down the middle. Kurt was young for such an accomplished businessman, having spent the last five years ruthlessly fighting his way to the top. Women turned to look at Kurt as he walked through the bar, but his expression scared them away quickly. It was his eyes; they were dark green and fierce.

The bar was mostly empty at six in the afternoon on a Tuesday. Kurt walked over to the counter and sat down on a grubby stool next to a man he didn't bother looking at. He didn't notice as the glances of women followed his path. He caught the eye of the bartender and signaled for a single shot of vodka, the first of many to come. Kurt sat silently at the bar, occasionally exchanging comments with the bartender. They had built up a casual rapport, thanks to Kurt's regular patronage. Kurt frequented this bar not because of the ambience or the drinks, but because it was the closest bar to his office.

It had been an hour since Kurt ordered his first shot when a woman with bright red hair walked in. Her head was turned away from Kurt as she headed toward a table of young men and women. Her red pea coat—a different shade than her hair—swung back and forth, and her black heels clicked loudly on the wood floor. She carried herself with confidence and something else that drew Kurt's attention.

"Liz," thought Kurt, his heart speeding up. He watched the woman eagerly as she made her way across the room. When she sat down, she finally turned her face in his direction.

Not Liz. Deflated, he looked away and turned his eyes down to stare at the counter of the mahogany bar.

Kurt didn't move from his bar stool for the rest of the night, except for the occasional trip to the men's room. He drank for hours. He stayed there until almost all the cabbies had already gone home for the night and the bartender called for last rounds.

As he got out of the shower, Kurt thought he saw what looked like a jet plane plummet past his window. He dashed to the window to see, but there was nothing there but the grassy landscape surrounding his condo building. Kurt shook his head to clear it and then walked back to his room to put on his black suit—his favorite of all. It was Armani and had cost him more than an average worker's monthly paycheck. Today was casual day at Kurt's office, but he wore the suit anyway. He made it a point always to look more professional than everyone else. Kurt grabbed his can opener and began to open a can of cat food while he scanned his apartment for a sign of his Siamese. Napoleon was nowhere to be found. He walked to the cat's bowl and filled it with food anyway. Napoleon had not shown his face in three days, but his food was gone every day, so the cat was still around somewhere—just avoiding him. Kurt had bought this cat for companionship, but no one had told Napoleon that was his job. Now the cat was no more than an extra food bill and the cause of a dirty litter box.

Before he left his condo, Kurt double checked his hair in the mirror to make sure the part was precisely down the middle. Satisfied with his appearance, he left his condo and took a taxi to work. It was not until he arrived that he realized he was almost an hour late. He strutted past the cubicles and into his office, no one daring to challenge him for being late. He sat at his desk facing one of his three bare walls and just missed seeing the clouds fall past his window.

Normally, Kurt worked hard once he got to the office, but not today. He idled away the time until lunch, filling out a few forms and shopping online for a new stainless steel coffee maker. He couldn't concentrate. His mind kept going back to the woman in Rum Bar with the bright red hair. She had looked so much like Liz.

Liz's red hair had been the first thing that caught Kurt's attention. It hung down to her waist and was as vivid as her shade of red lipstick—lipstick that left a bright red stain on the filter end of the white cigarette she smoked as she leaned lightly against the white brick walls of the apartment building. At first, she hadn't noticed Kurt standing near her, watching. She was distracted by something up in the sky, or perhaps an important thought. Confidence soaked the air around her. Kurt was so stunned by her appearance that he dropped the canvas he was holding.

As he bent over to pick up his art before dirt could stain the still-drying paint, she came over to him.

"Do you need help?"

She was even more stunning up close. She had clear blue eyes and a few freckles splattered across her pale skin.

"No… I… just lost my grip." Kurt's composure evaporated under her gaze. He hadn't the slightest idea what to say to her.

"Are you an artist?" she asked, as she crushed out the butt of her cigarette with the toe of her white sneaker.

"Yes. Well, trying to be."

The canvas was swiftly taken from Kurt's hands. Liz held it up and studied the painting.

"I like it," she said, as she handed it back to Kurt. "You haven't sold anything yet?"

"No. I work in an office part time, to pay the bills."

"I know how that goes. Well, see you around Mr. Artist."

Kurt was relieved when noon rolled around. He normally felt comfortable in his office; it was his second home. But he felt anxious today and needed to get outside.

Large drops of rain fell solemnly from the sky. The rain was a surprise, as there had not been a cloud in the sky when Kurt left his condo. He didn't like to be concerned with such trivial inconveniences as the weather, so he ignored the rain. He decided to get a bagel and turned left down Park. He was soaked to the bone in seconds and muttered curses to the sky.

Halfway to the bagel shop, Kurt stopped at a crosswalk. While waiting for the light to change, he turned to the little old lady on his left to complain about the rain. He was stopped short when he realized that the woman didn't have a drop of rain on her. She was not carrying an umbrella, either. She just stood there in her yellow top and skirt, smiling. Had the rain somehow missed her? Impossible! Kurt felt suddenly nauseous and quickly looked away from her. The light changed and he hurried across.

There was no line at the bagel shop. He placed his order with a pimple-faced kid who looked at Kurt with a confused expression as Kurt dripped on the floor. Kurt glowered at him as he collected his food. He ate his sandwich alone in a booth far from the windows.

By the time Kurt left the bagel store, the rain had stopped. He was relieved until he noticed that there were no puddles. He could not understand how, after all that rain, there wasn't a single puddle. His shoes made squishing noises as he walked, and his suit was still dripping at the cuffs.

Kurt hurried back to his office and closed the door, collapsing into his chair. His clothes were uncomfortably damp.

"What the hell is going on?" he asked himself out loud. It was not just the odd rainfall that was bothering Kurt. He had not felt like himself since the night before—not since the moment the red-haired woman had walked into the bar. She had made him remember the one person he spent all his time trying to forget: Liz.

It was almost a year since Kurt had moved into his new apartment. He now had 10 filled canvasses, layers of paint overlapping one another to form a completely new thought. They told a story for Kurt.

Liz became a friend. She would come over to Kurt's apartment periodically to see what he was creating. Kurt loved everything he came to learn about Liz: she didn't own a television; she had a deep passion for Edgar Allan Poe (once reading him "The Tell-Tale Heart" while he painted); she smoked American Spirits because they didn't test on animals;

she made her own clothes and sometimes she even modeled her new designs for Kurt.

They would sit on his balcony and drink coffee. Liz would smoke cigarettes and look at his latest paintings. She gave him the best compliments on each new canvas, never saying anything negative. She had no idea that she was the reason for his sudden inspiration.

There was one painting Kurt never showed Liz. It was a painting of her. He had spent days trying to get just the right shade of red for her hair. Kurt was planning to confess his love for Liz on the day the painting was finished.

Since meeting Liz, Kurt's commitment to his art had doubled. He was inspired by her. Even though he'd been offered several full-time positions at his workplace, Kurt turned them down. He didn't want to trade his precious time to make art for a larger paycheck. He sometimes felt there wasn't enough time in a day and not enough days in a year to create all the paintings that were manifesting inside him.

Kurt dried out at his desk for the rest of the day, doodling on a pad, unable to work. He did his best to ignore the extremely loud noises outside the building, which started around 3 p.m. By the time Kurt left his office for the day, at exactly 5 p.m., he'd convinced himself he was back to normal. Then he stepped outside.

Street lamps littered the road. Cars drove right over their lifeless metal bodies, crunching the shattered glass around them. Their tires refused to pop, as if the glass was not even there, and the lamps were just shadow. It was raining again, but everybody on the street was walking around dry, without umbrellas, while Kurt was once again getting soaked.

"I have to get out of this fucking rain," Kurt growled to himself. He hailed a cab and told the cabbie to take him to Rum Bar, even though it was only two blocks away.

"Why are you so wet, fella?" asked the cabbie.

Kurt didn't answer, and the cabbie took the hint. Thunder boomed. It sounded close. Kurt tried to keep his eyes from looking out the window, but he couldn't stop himself. The cab stopped at a light and birds began to fall from the sky: pigeons at first, and purple finches, robins and mourning doves. Then bigger ones: seagulls, hawks and crows. Kurt even saw a pelican plummet to the sidewalk. He was speechless. He expected the cabbie to swear or scream, but when the light changed, the cabbie continued driving as if nothing strange was happening.

When they got to the bar, Kurt threw a crumpled bill at the cabbie and rushed inside.

"Vodka," he said to the bartender, even before sitting down.

"You look like you had a rough one, Mr. Colveman," the bartender said, shaking his head sympathetically. As he poured Kurt's drink, he noticed the water dripping off his customer and pooling on the clean wooden floor, but he had been working behind the bar for a long time and he knew it would be bad for his tips if he asked questions, especially with a regular like Mr. Colveman.

Kurt quickly pounded his first drink. There were no windows in the bar, so he could not see the rain, but he could still hear the thunder. When the alcohol hit his bloodstream his anxiety eased a fraction. He ordered another and swiveled around to see who else was at the bar.

She was there again, the woman who looked so much like Liz. Or maybe she'd never left. She was eyeing Kurt, looking at him the way Liz had looked at him—with curiosity. That was how Liz had looked when he'd finally worked up the courage to show her the portrait he'd done of her.

❧

He hadn't slept that night or the night before. He'd stayed awake plotting out every word he would say to Liz when he gave her the painting. He hoped he wouldn't sound too cliché or like a bad Hollywood romance. He was ready; the painting was ready; now it was time.

When Kurt knocked on the door, it wasn't Liz who opened it. It was a man wearing a sleek suit, his brown hair parted down the middle. He stood silently in the doorway, waiting for Kurt to speak first.

"Who's at the door, babe?" Liz's voice called out from inside the apartment. She walked over to the doorway and wrapped her arms around the man.

"Oh, hey! Kurt, what are you doing here?"

Kurt didn't say a word. Liz was wearing a low-cut red dress and a necklace that he'd never seen on her before. It was gold and in the shape of a heart. It was set with more tiny diamonds than Kurt had ever seen in his life.

Liz noticed the canvas underneath Kurt's arm. "Oh, I'm sorry, Kurt, I can't look at your painting right now. Josh and I were just about to go to dinner. He bought me this necklace just for the occasion."

"Set me back a pretty penny," said the man named Josh, "but this lady's worth it. Plus, I just got me a big raise down at the office."

"I'll try to come by tomorrow to see your painting." Liz smiled as she closed the door.

"What was I thinking?" Kurt asked himself. "He gave

her diamonds, and all I could do was to make her some stupid painting."

❦

Kurt could not understand it. All the patrons of Rum Bar were acting completely normal. They were drinking martinis, talking and laughing with their companions. Did they not care about the birds cascading from the sky and the monstrous storm outside?

Kurt's fear doubled as the ceiling began to crumble. Huge slabs of concrete crashed down around him, mercilessly crushing tables, chairs, and even the cash register. Kurt whimpered and put his arms over his head, but the strangest thing was how the slabs missed all the customers, who showed no reaction at all to the concrete downpour. Kurt started screaming. He had to get out. He knocked over his stool as everyone turned to look at him. They stared as he ran out of the bar.

Outside was even worse. Twenty-story buildings shattered and glass and steel rained down. The sky above was black now, and starless. Helicopters hit the ground and sprayed metal around them. A rogue piece grazed Kurt's calf. A small trickle of blood seeped down his leg.

Kurt ran as quickly as he could, past women strolling with shopping bags and men on their cell phones, none of whom paid him any notice. He ran as billboards began to tumble down from their frames. He hadn't even gone a block when a particularly large one, for life insurance, knocked Kurt down and trapped him.

"Help!" he yelled at people walking down the street. They were oblivious to the destruction. They looked at him with pity and a twinge of fear as they skirted past him. Lightning sparked and lit up the hotel behind Kurt. The huge structure was shaking. It was about to fall.

Kurt tried with every bit of his strength to lift the billboard with the smiling woman off him. Its weight was too much. Trapped, Kurt looked up at the sun setting in the black sky. It was a brilliant sunset filled with the most beautiful reds, yellows and oranges that Kurt had ever seen, yet it was the red that hurt his heart. It was the exact red he had used to paint Liz's hair.

Kurt gave up painting that day. He threw away every canvas, including the one he had made of Liz.

The next day, Kurt went to work and accepted the promotion and the raise that his boss had offered months ago. Then he poured himself into his job. Kurt worked hard. Every minute of his time was dedicated to the task. It didn't take long before he was offered another promotion and then another. His empty apartment filled with new appliances, a big-screen TV and well-made suits. He rarely saw Liz. Their only exchanges were brief greetings in the hallway or coming in or out of the building. Kurt was still completely in love with her, but it hurt too much to see her.

One day, Kurt's new, expensive appliances would no longer fit in his small, shabby apartment. After a week of condo hunting, he found the perfect place, and it was big enough for two. He decided it was time.

After signing the lease, he went to a jewelry shop—one of the very best in the world. He found a white-gold tennis bracelet inlayed with perfect, small diamonds. A week of his salary was spent on this overly extravagant gift, which was wrapped in pink tissue paper and placed in a small red box with a bow on top.

Kurt rehearsed over and over again what he would say to Liz when she opened the door. The words fled when he saw her face.

"Liz, I love you," he said.

"Oh, Kurt," a smile creased her lips.

"I brought you this." He handed her the box. She slowly began to unwrap it. Now that his secret was out, he found himself blurting out everything in a rush.

"I'm moving out of this dump. I've got a great-paying job. I make buckets of cash now telling other people what to do. Come with me, I'll take care of you. I'll give you anything you want."

Liz wasn't looking at him. She was looking down at the bracelet.

"What is this?" she asked, her voice low and unhappy.

"It's a bracelet, Liz; it's white-gold and diamonds. Only the finest."

"What the hell happened to you?" she screamed, her face twisted with disappointment. "What happened to my sweet, starving artist who used to show me his beautiful artwork?" Her eyes filled with tears. "I don't even know who you are now!"

"Liz," Kurt began to plead. "I'm better now. I was never going to get anywhere as an artist. I have money now, a new television. I've got everything."

"No, you don't Kurt. You've lost it all." Liz threw the bracelet, box and all, back at Kurt. Tears streamed down her cheeks. "Goodbye, Kurt."

She pushed him out and the door closed in Kurt's face. He shoved the bracelet and box into his pocket and walked back to his apartment. He packed up all his belongings and moved out the next day. Kurt never saw Liz again.

Lying on the sidewalk, three tons of weight on his chest, Kurt knew this was the end. In a matter of seconds, the hotel, which was shaking violently, would succumb and he would be buried beneath thousands of pounds of bricks and mortar. Kurt Riley Colveman would disappear from the world.

"Liz, I'm so sorry," he mumbled, tears of regret leaking out of his eyes. "I never should have given up my art. I never should have wasted my life doing meaningless work to make money."

A cardinal landed beside Kurt. He watched it flit back and forth picking up small crumbs from the cracks in the sidewalk. The bird turned and looked sadly at Kurt. Then it lifted off, leaving behind a single red feather.

Happy

Every day, it was the first thing I would see when I woke up. And, goddamn it, I have always hated waking up.

Every single day at exactly six in the freaking morning, my alarm clock would go off. It made the worst noise. *Twerp! Twerp! Twerp!* My wife picked it out, obviously. I have hated her a little bit ever since she brought it home. If you hit snooze, it would go off again two minutes later. The damn thing was persistent as hell. And my wife would prod me sharply in the back with her pointer finger every time it went off, which didn't help a bit with my feelings about her.

So every two minutes *twerp!* prod, *twerp!* prod. It was enough to drive any somewhat sane man at least partially nuts. Eventually, I would forgo my attempts to fall back asleep, being quiet so as not disturb my now-pretending-to-sleep wife, I would push down the covers and open my eyes.

And there he would be. The jackass never took a day off. Not one, the goddamn dwarf. I don't mean dwarf as in a little person. No, this was an actual dwarf: hideous kelly-green pants, ridiculous slouchy brown hat, and a huge goddamn smile on his face. At first, I mistook him for a gnome, but I researched it a bit and gnomes have white beards. His is red. He's definitely a dwarf. As if that's not bad enough, this dwarf holds a sign in his grubby little hands, always the same sign. "Happy" it says, in big, shiny, gold letters. He used some sparkly paint when he made it. I'm sure he's the one who made it, the jackass.

The first few times I woke to his goddamn smile and sign, I let out a little shriek. Come on—it's not something you expect to see first thing when you open your eyes.

I would throw my legs out of bed and rub my eyes—not that it ever helped—and the dwarf would still be there. Sometimes, I would hurl a pillow at it. He would always dodge it, the little jerk.

"Stop throwing pillows!" my wife would say bitterly. She was a bitch. I tried to divorce her at least a hundred times. When I found that I couldn't say the words, I tried to write them down. The goddamn dwarf would always take the paper away from me. I would write a letter telling her that I was leaving her and place it on the kitchen table. If I turned around and turned back only half a second later, the letter would be gone. The dwarf would be in the exact same place as before, but he'd be chewing on bits of paper with my handwriting scribbled on them. He would smile, wider even than usual, when he swallowed.

That was the only time I would see him chewing on any-thing, so maybe he lived off paper full of hatred. I had tried giving him food a couple of times, not that I would have cared if he had starved—it was only out of curiosity. But the dwarf wouldn't touch a thing.

I tried packing a suitcase and leaving without saying a word, but the suitcase, which was brand new and designer made, broke. The bottom simply fell out. Like that, the dwarf kept me stuck in my dreadful marriage. Completely and utterly stuck for seven years.

That dwarf had no sense of privacy, either! He followed me into the bathroom and wouldn't avert his eyes when I peed. Same thing in the shower.

He would perch on the toilet, top down, with his legs dangling, swinging them to and fro, his hands resting on his lap, and his smile never once leaving his lips. I would usually try to cover myself as I got out of the shower. But after a while I thought, "Fuck it!" I got used to him. If he wanted to watch, what did I care? I could be having sex with my wife, on one of those rare occasions, and he wouldn't even avert his eyes. The smile never changed.

That smile was the worst part. Did I mention that ever since that asshole started following me around I haven't been able to frown? Not once. I would feel like I'm frowning. I would look into the mirror and see myself frowning, but to everybody else I was always smiling. And I couldn't yell or get really angry. If I tried, not a single word would come out.

I would never open the door or even unlock it for him, but every day when I sat in the driver's seat of my Honda, there he was in the passenger seat beside me. He somehow got himself buckled in and everything. I tried to trick him. I'd get in, get out, start walking; the guy never fell for a thing.

I could tell he liked the car ride the best because I like to listen to the radio. The second the music started, he would start bopping along in that creepy, silent way he has. Not once in the six or seven years he'd been following me did he utter a single word. But that didn't mean he couldn't communicate. When I tried to turn off the music, he would stare directly at me, not losing his smile. In those moments his smile suddenly seemed to hold the essence of something very sinister. His eyes would bore into me, and I couldn't stand it. I always turned the music back on. Then he'd go back to his chair dancing, his body shaking and butt wiggling. His sense of rhythm was actually decent, for a dwarf.

Nobody else could see the little twerp; only me. He followed me everywhere at work, even when I went to lunch or had a meeting in my boss's office. When I sat at my desk, there he would be, holding Happy in front of me. Wherever I was, he was sitting across from me, standing behind me or next to me. If I started talking to people, he liked to stand behind them, reach his arms high and hold the goddamn sign up above their heads.

Normally, after work I would simply head home, dwarf in tow. I wouldn't ask to go out with my coworkers, and I noticed none of them ever invited me to happy hour. Instead, I would eat the bland meals that my wife unceremoniously put in front of me. Then I would sit in front of the television, ignoring the dwarf in front of the screen, until I fell asleep.

And that's how it was, every day, until I put a stop to it.

Twerp! Twerp! Twerp! Prod. *Twerp! Twerp! Twerp!* Prod. It was mid-winter, about seven years since that dwarf had started following me around. I hit snooze. Two minutes later. *Twerp! Twerp! Twerp!* Prod.

I briefly wondered how it could be that the goddamn sign had not lost a speck of glittery gold metallic paint in the past seven years. I'd never seen him repaint it. I wouldn't have been surprised if it was some kind of creepy dwarf magic.

He smiled. I frowned. And then I threw a pillow at him and missed, as usual.

"How many fucking times do I have to tell you to stop throwing those goddamn pillows!" said my lovely wife.

I turned my head to face her. I didn't say a word. "And stop smiling!" I could feel the frown lines in my face but I knew I was smiling. "It must be at least seven years since I've seen you frown. Why are you always smiling? You smile all the time. And you hardly ever talk," said my wife with great frustration. "Why!?"

I would have loved to tell her that she was a frigid bitch and I hated her goddamn guts, but I couldn't. I just smiled at her and got out of bed to get ready for work.

On the way to work that day, I turned on the heavy metal station. I hated heavy metal, but I figured even the dwarf couldn't really enjoy it.

I was wrong. He started head-banging along. He was really getting into it. And for some reason, his hat stayed on his head the whole time. I quickly changed it to classical.

When we pulled into the parking lot, I wished more than ever that I could somehow just lock the little bastard in the car and not have to see him until the end of the day, or ever again, but he somehow unlocked the door and hopped right after me. I didn't bother trying to run; I'd learned a long time ago how fast he is.

"Wipe that smile off your face," my boss said with irritation when he saw me walk through the door. "The corporate auditor is coming today, and I need you to look serious for once." The dwarf was standing right behind my boss. I couldn't see him right then, but Happy was hovering right above my boss's head. My boss definitely did not look happy. I nodded, and he walked away.

"Damn it! Today is not going to be fun," I thought.

About an hour into my shift, the auditor came into my cubicle, my boss following at his heels.

"Oh, there is nothing really interesting to see here," my boss was saying to the auditor. "This is just one of our clerks doing routine paperwork." That about summed up my job. But the auditor seemed pretty keen to check out my cubicle.

"And what are you doing here, my boy?" asked the gray-haired auditor with the straight mouth.

I briefly explained my job to him. I won't explain it here. I wouldn't want to bore you to death.

"You seem to enjoy your job," remarked the auditor. I had to hold back my laughter.

I simply nodded.

"Is there anything that you wish you could change about the company?"

I could see my boss frown in the background. I shook my head.

"Come on, boy, don't be shy. Name one thing you would like to change."

The dwarf chose this moment to become even more distracting, standing directly between me and the auditor and hopping from one foot to the other shaking Happy. I resolved myself to point at something. But, before I could decide what to point at, my boss yelled at me. "Come on, say something!"

I pointed at him. Damn! I knew I'd fucked up.

The auditor's eyes widened in surprise. "Alright, on to the next one, then," he said, and they let me be.

Well, that was it. I knew I had really screwed up this time. I glared at the dwarf and got to work.

I tried not to think of all the bullshit that would inevitably follow. I droned though my paperwork, rubbing the annoying stress knot in my neck.

A few hours later I heard my boss saying goodbye to the auditor. As soon as the door closed after him, he came straight back to my cubicle.

"My office," was all he said.

I got out of my chair and followed my boss to the back of

the building. The dwarf tagged along swinging Happy back and forth. I stepped into my boss's office and he slammed the door behind me.

"What the fuck were you trying to pull?" he asked me. I didn't say a word. "Give me an answer right this minute!"

"Nothing," I manage to mumble. "Accident."

"Accident!" he yelled at the top of his voice. "Accident! Get the hell out of my building. You are fired. I am so god-damn sick of your fucking smile!"

I didn't move. I knew I wouldn't be able to get another job, not as long as I had this smile on my face. I was fucked. I wouldn't be able to pay rent or buy food. I had a brief picture of myself dressed in rags huddled on a street corner with a sign and this same goddamn smile on my face. The dwarf moved from the side of me to right in front of me, holding Happy out to me. This was all his goddamn fault.

I was standing right next to my now-former boss's desk. On top of it lay a sharp, silver letter opener, looking as if it had been placed there just for me. I knew this time, some-how, I wouldn't miss. I grabbed it, not listening anymore to my boss yelling at me. I lunged at the dwarf, aiming straight for his heart, and this time I didn't miss.

A scream filled the room, high-pitched and louder than any human noise I had ever heard. He dropped Happy to the floor and collapsed into a crumpled, dwarf-shaped ball. Red, red blood poured through the dwarf's shirt to stain the mellow yellow carpet of the office.

I looked up, surprised to see my former boss's shocked expression. He was staring directly at the now dead dwarf.

"What the fuck...? Who the hell..?" was all he could muster.

The office door opened, and in walked building security.

"It was him!" yelled my former boss, pointing at me. "He killed the little guy! The little guy came from nowhere, and he killed him!"

They spared no mercy with their handcuffs, digging them as tightly into my wrists as they possibly could. I could feel the cold metal cutting into my skin, but it wasn't all I could feel. My mouth's muscles were clenched tightly into a smile. I never used to feel the smile before. I did now, and it hurt. I looked at my reflection in the window as the police dragged me out. It was grotesque, the smile—wide and pink. My gums were showing, and each one of my teeth was bared. I was terrified looking at my own face.

I wasn't in jail for very long before they sent me to the asylum. Nobody ever questioned where the dwarf came from and whether or not he was human. From what I understand, he was buried as a John Doe. I don't know what happened to Happy.

To this day, the smile has still not left my face. It's permanent—a part of me now. All the other patients call me Smiley. But otherwise it's not too bad here. My wife doesn't visit. She just sends her lawyer with divorce papers. I don't sign them. I want to, but I can't; something won't let me. It doesn't matter because I never have to see her, and it's not like I'm about to meet a new woman any time soon. The dwarf is gone, which is the most important part of this story. It's been two years since last I saw him—dead. For a while I thought for sure he'd come back—dwarf magic and all that—or that another one would show up to take his place. But no, he's gone. No more Happy.

About the Author

Kerri Hewitt is a writer currently residing in Portland, Oregon. She grew up in Tucson, Arizona, where she studied Creative Writing and Spanish at the University of Arizona. In her free time, Kerri enjoys making art, reading, and getting involved in human rights and animal rights causes. On a typical day she can be found typing away in a coffee shop, chowing down at a potluck, or imbibing some of Portland's finest microbrews while dreaming up plots for new stories.

www.ingramcontent.com/pod-product-compliance
Lightning Source LLC
Chambersburg PA
CBHW030636130626
46552CB00002B/884